# OUTLAW
# BLOOD

# OUTLAW
# BLOOD

## NOAH J. MATTHEWS

The Pearl

PEARLBOOKS.CC

DEVELOPMENTAL EDITOR
Brad Pauquette & Vella Karman

COPY EDITOR
Thirzah

BOOK DESIGNER
R.J. Catlin

COVER ARTIST
Levi Matthews

PAPERBACK ISBN: 978-1-960230-13-3
EBOOK ISBN: 978-1-960230-14-0

LIBRARY OF CONGRESS CONTROL NUMBER: 2025931417

To everyone who's found respite only by falling face down on the endless, blazing sands at the foot of the Sandwalker.

Also to Bob Quantum. He's made so much possible.

———

They say the life of an outlaw ain't worth a pint of milk, but I'll bet my neck they don't value their own lives so little...

# ONE

# THE OUTLAW

THE CRESCENT MOON hung low in the sky, coiled above the distant mountains like a snake preparing to strike. The wind sent a few lonely tumbleweeds across the desert toward their uncertain destination. Down in the valley—rounded like it had been scooped out with a spoon—an outlaw tread a dusty path toward the ramshackle town of Annaday. His head was down, no bandanna or wide-brimmed hat to conceal his identity. A jacket the color of dried blood hung from his shoulders.

The dark-skinned outlaw paused, boots scraping to a stop on the dry sand. The flickering moonlight inched down at him, glinting off the revolver at his hip. He inhaled the parched desert air.

That sent him into a coughing fit.

He pounded his chest. "Kein!" he swore, "We haven't had a grain-shot in over a week!"

The outlaw took a shallow breath through his nose. The violence in his chest died down a little.

He turned his eyes toward the moonlit town. The shacks

and shops stamped a vague circle on the sand, Main Street cleaving it just off-center. Right on the edge of Annaday, directly in front of the outlaw, sat a little cottage—white paint peeling, wood shingles sparse, a broad and familiar porch, and a white-fenced yard as pretty and grassy as cemetery grounds.

The outlaw smiled. *No one grows plants like Ma.*

He straightened, lifted his hand to the mass of tight black curls on his head. It'd been a year since he'd committed a major crime. His parents would be safe—no danger, no lawmen—safe.

The outlaw strode forward with short, quiet steps. He came to the squat white fence, jumped it, landing silently on the grass. With a glance toward the other shacks, he crossed the yard and tiptoed onto the porch to avoid his spurs clicking. He raised his hand to knock on the door, hesitated, then rapped his knuckles against the wooden frame.

Some rustling sounded from within like the hiss of ghostly dresses. The outlaw knocked again. Footsteps. The outlaw held his breath.

The door opened, creaking as it always had. A short lady stood in the doorway, holding a tin lamp. She wore a blue calico dress. Curly black hair hung around her face, almost as dark-skinned as his own. Deep wrinkles framed her eyes, and her mouth turned downward in a frown.

The outlaw held his breath. "Ma," he whispered.

The older lady squinted, then drew in a breath herself. "Clye?"

Clye wrapped his mother in a hug, his muscular arms hard against her back. Silence passed a moment. It had been too long since he'd seen her—his ma, the wife of his pa.

Ma patted her son's back. "That's enough, Lyle."

Clye stiffened, drew back from his ma. Lines crossed his face that had only recently grown out of its childish roundness. "What the hona, Ma? You're teasing," he said.

The wavering light of the lamp glistened off his mother's eyes. Anger? Joy?

Clye cleared his throat. "'Lyle Yeller' really is a name, isn't it? Just rolls off the tongue."

"Mm-hmm. Let's take this conversation inside. I ain't the only one with ears in this town."

They slipped in the door, and Ma shut it behind them. She strode to the rickety wooden table in the center of the room and set the lamp down on it. The orange beams licked every corner of their little cottage—the iron stove to the right, the rug dark as scorpion blood, the white curtain in the back of the cottage that hid Ma and Pa's bed from view.

Ma sat down in a chair at one end of the table, Clye at the other.

"Haven't seen much of you, son."

"Ma, I wanted to see you and Pa every single day since I left—"

"Ten years ago."

"I wrote! And visited."

"Twice, Clye. You seen us twice in ten years. Not that I don't appreciate you lookin' out for our safety."

Clye drummed his fingers on the table. Three deep scars marked his index finger—sign of the Yeller gang. Ma reached out and covered his hand with her wrinkled one. Clye looked up into her blue eyes.

No smile hung on her lips. "I just pray you ain't the same man that's printed on the wanted posters."

Clye lowered his eyes. "Me too, Ma…" His muscles tensed. "That's why I'm here. I wanna stay with you—earn my name

3

back. I'll get me a good job—something respectable like a cowboy—and—"

"Clye, the Law." His mother's frown had deepened, lines marring her forehead.

Clye clenched his fists, pulled his hand from beneath his ma's. *I can't run no more,* he thought. He'd run for so long—dodging the Law, trying to live right and redeem his name somehow. But nothin'—nobody cared. Except his ma and pa. When Clye read their letters he could feel their love pulsing through like an injured heart still beating. He wanted to be back—back under the shade of their love instead of fighting tooth and nail for his worth in the blistering heat.

He looked over at his ma—noticed the narrowed eyes, the pinched lips, the trembling hands.

"I'm gonna have to earn my name somewhere else, ain't I?" he said.

Ma nodded. "Find some girl like Annie Daluwen—marry some money—"

"Ma, you know I've never been marriage material."

Ma shrugged. "Still, you could try."

Clye shook his head. He looked at his mother. "I wish I could stay," he said. His hand started to tremble. "I'll go east—my record should be clear there. I'll go to church, get a job, and—"

"You can't be a cowboy."

Clye's chest tightened. *Pa would say I could.* "It's been years since I've committed a crime—no one's out looking for me. In the east no one would know who Clye Galler is."

Ma sighed. She looked her son in the eyes. "Baby I think I'm the only ma in Drode who c'n say this with love—you're a

4

stain on our family name." A smile tugged at her lips. "If your Pa wasn't sleepin' so well, I'd wake him up so he could tell you how proud of you he is."

She gripped his hand harder. "Takes guts to redeem your name."

Clye nodded, scratched a dry patch of skin on his arm. It'd been so long since he'd seen his parents—so long that he'd waited for this moment. And now he had to leave.

"I'm gonna say goodbye to Pa," he said. His mother let go of his hand as he rose to his feet.

Clye walked across the floor to the embroidered white curtain, his soft leather boots quiet against the floorboards, and muffled more by the rug. The serpent pattern embossed into the leather of his boots stood out, dark in the orange light. Clye stopped a pace away from the curtain, straightened. His eyes followed the pattern of birds and tree leaves stitched into the curtain's fabric—fat little birds with wind and song flowing out of their beaks. It'd been years since he'd seen a bird like that. Buzzards and mountain igrus were his more frequent companions. Kein it'd been a long ten years. Clye shook his head, reached up and jangled the curtain-hooks—once, twice, in the traditional fashion. He'd never forgotten.

A little groan came from within.

"Who is it? Mary? I'll protect you."

"It's our son," called Ma.

"Oh…"

Clye parted the curtain, left it open. His father lay on the straw mattress, head propped up with some patchwork pillows Ma had sewn together out of bits of cloth—love in pieces. His father's face was round and bald, with piercing, smiling eyes.

"Haven't seen you in a minute, son," he said.

Clye knelt beside the bed and looked up at his dad like he'd do when he was young and short and wanting to play "cowboy" all day. He couldn't help from tearing up. "You always stuck by me, Pa," he whispered.

His father toyed with the edge of the blanket with wrinkled fingers. His eyes looked sunken, watery. Then he coughed, smiling weakly. "I love you, son—outlaw or no."

Clye hugged his father—tried to keep the tears from spilling out. A moment felt like the afterlife. Heat pulsed up from his dad's face, skin, even through the blanket—unnatural heat. Clye let go and stood up. "Pa, you ain't hot under there?"

"He'll be fine," interrupted his mother. Clye turned to see her standing by the door like a shadowed guardian. "I'll see you out," she said.

Clye nodded, patted his father on the shoulder, turned, and went to the door. His mother unlocked it and pushed him gently out. Clye smiled. He turned to say goodbye, but the door was closed.

He paused a moment, brow furrowed, lips pursed. He slowly turned, looking out from the porch onto the little grassy yard, clean as a graveyard in the moonlight.

He sighed. *Better get going,* he thought, and stepped down off the porch.

He marched out through his mother's green yard, over her pretty white fence, and out into the open desert. It was a good night for walking—so cool and clear that Clye would've taken off his boots to feel the sand between his toes—but he wasn't that stupid. In the day, direct contact with the sand would cause the blood to boil. At night, it'd dehydrate the body bit by bit, from the toes up to the crown. By the time it got to your thighs and your knees started to ache, your feet would be dry and shriveled as a nawfa carcass. No, Clye wasn't that stupid.

Clye adjusted his jacket over his shoulders, feeling his short sword clank against his shirt buttons. He walked east, his shoulder to the distant mountain ridge tracing a line all the way round Drode's equator, like a noose around a neck.

THE MOON SANK into the west. Clye guessed he'd been traveling four hours dead east over the dry sand. He paused and scratched the stubble on his chin, thinking.

"Need to make camp," he said.

He opened the right flap of his jacket. Inside was a pocket stuffed with a palm-sized roll of salra—soft mountain plant stalks woven together into a mat. Clye pulled out the salra and unfurled it onto the sand—the folds shook out into a mat just long and wide enough for him to lay on. He laid the mat gently on the sand.

Carefully, Clye got down on his hands and knees and crawled onto the salra. He turned awkwardly onto his back, the soft mat a thin barrier between him and the sand. As every Drodite is taught, he crossed one leg over the other, shut his eyes, and covered his face with his arms, tucking his hands into the pockets sewn into the shoulders of his jacket.

The wind kicked a spray of sand over the outlaw, but he didn't move. Didn't sneeze. Steady breathing and keeping the face and feet covered were the only ways to survive a night in Drode.

As he lay there, Clye let a prayer escape his lips—a rehearsed symbol of a faith all but forgotten—"Sandwalker, keep the blood within my body, keep the heart within my chest, keep the dreams within my eyelids, and guard my name with your whirlwinds."

A thought followed the heels of that prayer like a lonely child clawing at his mother's dress, *Guard my name, 'cause I've lost it*. A tear escaped his eyelid, slid down his nose and wet his lips.

"Guard my *name*." The words came out in a gasp, and sleep claimed him.

## TWO
# BEGGAR'S BOWL

CLYE SLEPT LATE. His eyes flickered open to the blinding light of the mid-morning sun. Heat soaked his body, sweat soaked his breeches.

"Kein!" he cursed, and leaped to his feet. Dizziness engulfed him and he yanked his hands out of his shoulder pockets, putting his arms out to steady himself. Steps left, steps right, back left again, his confused legs finally came to a halt. Clye shook his head and rubbed the sand out of his eyes.

"If only I had a mount," he murmured, stooping down again to roll up the salra. Even as a boy Clye had seen the cowboys on their scaly steeds and dreamed of trekking sand and stone on one. Shame the Yeller Gang only went on foot—"stealth" they said.

He stuffed the salra into the right flap of his jacket, squinted at the mountains to the north, turned his shoulder to them, and walked east.

He'd never been to the eastern towns, but he'd heard names—Jute, Crayridge, Valkar, Capital Young where the Congress met.

*I'll run into Jute in a few days*, he told himself. He hadn't had a drop to drink in days.

THE MARKET ON the corner of Jute was stagnant for all its color. Bright banners hung from the stalls, embroidered with the names of the wares within. A handful of villagers ambled through the street, eyes on the ground—away from the afternoon sun. Carcasses hung from the butcher shop, meat sizzled on the spits of street vendors. It was death, not life, that Jute sold.

Under an orange banner, a street vendor turned his meat-laden skewer over a small fire.

The wind blew a tumbleweed down the street and past the vendor. Behind the tumbleweed stumbled Clye, skin flaming after another day of travel under the Drodite sun. Yesterday had been an exhausting trek over the sand, and this morning he had again woken up late. He was lucky he made it to Jute alive. He walked over to the vendor, whose head was wrapped in a gray bandanna.

"Howdy," Clye said, head swimming with the heat.

"Howdy," answered the vendor without looking up. "I got some wild-caught nawfa here—you want me to set you up with a steak or two? I'll throw in some sauce, family recipe."

"Might if I had money," Clye forced a chuckle. "You got a well in this here town?"

The vendor jerked his head up the street. "Follow the street up yonder. It's in the square. Two kaj for a bucket if you're a stranger."

"Ah. Well, good day."

"Sandwalker guard your name," the vendor returned dryly.

Clye's chest tightened. *Haven't heard that phrase in a while. These eastern folks.*

He walked up the street, past the smells seducing his pinched stomach. He emerged into the town square and froze.

A massive gallows stood in the center of the square. The platform was made of obsidian, ringed with torch sconces. The rest was a porous gray stone painted all over with red swirls and letters—curses against the lawbreakers. The traditional crimson rope hung from the gallows' single outstretched arm. From the rope hung a corpse, swinging gently in the breeze, blood coating an open mouth and empty eye sockets. Half-rotten intestines dangled from the corpse's drawn torso like ribbons of morbid celebration.

Clye lowered his eyes. It had been too long since he'd been in a square. They were all the same. Hona, he should've remembered!

Clye skirted the gallows, trying to ignore the buzz of flies that appraised him as he passed. The well—tall and built from the smashed corpses of boulders—squatted at the far end of the square. It was shaded by a large wooden shack with tar-and-sand roofing. A thick embroidered banner hung above the door, the wind tugging futilely at the edges. "Law House," the banner read.

"Kein," Clye breathed.

A man in a wide-brimmed hat stood beside the well, elbow resting on its wooden cover. A bucket sat at his feet. Clye could tell he was a lawman by the blue cloth sewn onto the left side of his jacket. Clye inhaled, stepped forward.

"Howdy," he said.

The lawman turned toward him with heavy-lidded eyes.

"Howdy, stranger," he said. "You lookin' to get a drink?"

"Yessir," Clye answered, bowing stiffly.

"It'll be…" the lawman blinked. "You just want a sip?"

"That'll keep me goin' for the moment," Clye answered.

"Where's your hat? Don't look much like a beggar to me."

"Someone stole it." *It's the truth.*

The lawman scratched his chin. "Well, you just get yourself to the hatter before all of Jute sees you bareheaded. Thank the Sandwalker it ain't a holy day."

He shook his head, stooped and grabbed the bucket. With his free hand the lawman slid the well cover off and onto the sand. He clipped the bucket handle onto the hook, fed the rope into the well. When he cranked the bucket up again, the lawman pulled a ladle from his belt, filled it, and offered it to Clye.

"Much obliged," Clye said, downing the ladleful of water. He couldn't help but sigh afterward. The cool liquid wet his lips, tongue, and throat in one exhilarating rush. Kein, if only he had money, he'd do it over and over again until he downed the whole bucket, satisfying the thirsty hole inside.

Clye handed the ladle back to the lawman and bowed.

"Sandwalker guard your name," he said, turning and crossing the square, eyes down, the soft *creak* of the red rope loud as a scream in his ears.

Clye walked back onto the market street. He scanned the banners. *Ah.* The white banner of the hatter waved gently above a doorless wooden shack. Clye straightened. A hat was the first step to respectability, and washing the blood from his name. He nodded to himself, then walked across the street to the doorway of the hatter's shop.

He knocked on the doorpost.

"Come in," croaked an old, dry voice.

Clye entered the shack. It was dark enough that his eyes took a moment to adjust. An old man hunched over a stool, sewing two bits of leather together. A squat table sat beside him. Hats lined the right wall of the shack, tools the left. It was too dark to see the far wall. The old man on the stool had his sleeves rolled up above his elbows, and a pointed white hat perched on his head. The old man looked up at Clye, blue eyes squinted, face framed by a massive white beard and mustache.

"Repair, career, or pleasure?" the hatter said.

Clye scratched the back of his head. "Uh, lawman at the well said it was for decency."

"Ah." The hatter chuckled. "Can't be seen in church without one. Well, sir, what's your profession?"

Clye paused, chest tight. "Cowboy," he said. "I'm a cowboy."

"Good money in that business," the hatter nodded. He set the bits of leather he was stitching on the table. He struggled to his feet and held out his hand to Clye.

Clye licked his lips. "I ain't got no money. Is decency costly?"

"Your license, sir—your ranching license from the Law— can't be a cowboy without one."

"I'm a stranger in town."

The hatter's brow furrowed like the wrinkled pages of a lawbook. "You still have a license."

Clye felt sweat on his forehead, though it was quite cool in the shop. "I-I lost it."

The hatter remained immovable. "I'm not handin' out eight hundred kaj of material to an unlicensed stranger."

"But the lawman said—"

"No license, no hat. Now get the kein outta here. Sandwalker guard your name, *kive*."

Clye licked his lips. *Hona! Can't escape, can't escape it.*

He bowed to the hatter, turned and walked outside.

The late afternoon sun beamed down on Clye's head. He kicked a tumbleweed as it passed, sending it flying in a shower of sand grains.

"Alms, sir? Alms?"

Clye looked to his right. A beggar sat against the siding of the hat shop, holding up a wooden bowl. Clye knelt down on the sand in front of the beggar.

"Ain't got money," he said, "but we could make a deal. You get me a hat, I'll give you a sword."

The beggar's eyes glowed in their sunken sockets. He scratched his beard with his free hand. "What kinda sword is she?"

Clye opened the left flap of his jacket and pulled out his short sword—it was about the length of his forearm, with a broad, silver blade. The guard wrapped around the leather handle like a waiting serpent.

The beggar's eyes grew wide.

"Oh," he said, "Oh."

"You like it?" Clye said.

"I could eat for a month on that thing," the beggar said, "or kill the kives who spit on me."

Clye smiled. These were the men he was used to—hard. "You can get me a hat?"

The beggar looked left and right like he was about to share some dreadful secret. "*Grain.* Throw in a grain-shot and I'll find you a hat, mister."

Clye dug his knee into the sand at his feet. "Looks like plenty of grain right here to me."

The beggar wrinkled his nose. "That stuff's fine for bringin' a sandstorm to its knees, but for feelin' up—" he patted his cheek "—I need the *real* stuff. You know—fine white western—"

"I know." Clye held up a finger. He sheathed the sword inside his jacket and yanked a bag from the pocket of his breeches. The lumpy bag smiled up at him like the face of his bald father. "I was savin' this for hard times, but…"

He undid the string that held the bag closed and poured half of its contents into the beggar's bowl.

The beggar grinned a toothless smile. "Much obliged," he said, and threw a pinch of the sand in his mouth. He swallowed slowly.

Clye smiled. Amateurs chewed—bad for the teeth. But veterans in the Way of Sand swallowed—slowly, savoring every grain of sand.

The beggar's deep-set brown eyes widened, and a lazy smile slithered across his face. "Much obliged," he repeated, slouching back against the shack.

"You'll get me a hat by sundown?" Clye said.

The beggar threw another pinch in his mouth, closed his eyes. "Good stuff," he murmured.

"Kein!" Clye swore, jumping to his feet and stuffing the bag in his pocket. He wasn't getting a hat out of this. He kicked some sand at the beggar and marched farther up the market street.

"I'll get you your hat, mister." The beggar's vice had grown high and wavery.

THAT NIGHT CLYE hunkered down in a little alley hugging the saloon on the east side of Jute. He spread his salra next to the brick foundation and covered his face, whispering his prayer. "Guard my name. Guard my name…"

He wished he could have stayed with his parents—but he couldn't afford to put them in danger. If they were dead, they couldn't love him.

Somehow he'd redeem his name. The name of Clye Galler would be a name of honor, a name to live on in family and crimson embroidery. The name of Lyle Yeller would be buried forever—under the hot and secret sands.

# THREE
# ANGORAETH

"HEY, KID—YOU KNOW that's my saloon you're sleeping against? You havin' a good dream, or what?" A chuckle. "You know I'm gonna have to ask you to leave. Beggars aren't welcome at my saloon—no offense. Unless they can pay, of course."

Clye's eyelids flew open. A short, pale-skinned man stood over him, smoking a cigar. Clye ripped his hands from his pockets and drew his pistol.

Shorty chuckled, pulled a gold watch from his bulging waistcoat. "Well, I'm about two minutes and fifteen seconds from bringin' down the Law on you—you fine with that?"

"I'll shoot you." The words slipped out unbidden from Clye's mouth. Kein old habits!

Shorty tucked his watch back into his waistcoat and adjusted the soft gray lapels of his suit. Clye noticed the bowler hat perched on the man's head. Bowler hats were the mark of people in the saloon business—their managers, bartenders, jesters.

Shorty sighed, sending a puff of smoke into the air. "Beggars are feisty," his hand dropped to his hip.

Clye kept his pistol trained on the pale-skin, noticed the curve of a pistol grip tucked under the bulge of the man's side.

"I'm a powerful man," Shorty droned, cigar still in his mouth. His hand curled around his pistol grip. "If you killed me, a lot of people would be unhappy. Plus you'd hang for murder."

Now was not the time to risk a shootout. Clye's heart pounded as he racked his mind. Then the horrible thought came to him. "What if I'm a bounty hunter?" he said.

Clye kept his voice cool, even, *proud*. That pride—that fiercely quiet haughtiness—was what every bounty hunter carried. Because they knew that, unlike outlaws, they would not be put to death for their crimes. *Kives*.

Shorty laughed. "You're not a hunter—certainly not guild, anyway. You haven't followed a single keining rule of bounty hunting etiquette—and believe me, sir, I *know* all the rules."

"What do you want?"

The laughter left Shorty's eyes. "I've already told you." He removed his cigar. "Let me rephrase it as advice. *Don't* sleep by saloons, and *don't* get caught on a holy day without a hat. Bad for the image, bad for business." With a wink, the man walked away.

Clye fell back against his salra mat, pistol-hand splashing down on the sand. He closed his eyes. Hona he hated himself! Five years after the Yeller gang broke apart, and *still* he felt like an outlaw. Talked like an outlaw. Acted like an outlaw.

Moisture on his eyelashes. A deep feeling of filthiness staining his soul. *Redeem my name.* Clye wiped his face on his sleeve and holstered his pistol. Got to his feet, rolled up the salra, and tucked it into his jacket.

*Church.* He'd been a kid last time he went, but he remembered liking it. The whole town singing, then listening to a string of words they couldn't understand. There was something mysterious about it—a primal connection to each other like all were children of one father, or all had inhaled the same sand.

All upstanding citizens went to church.

Clye walked out of the alley.

HE FOUND THE CHURCH on the far end of town: a massive, lonely lump of white marble with a wooden dome crowning it. A golden crescent was tacked onto a little spire projecting upward from the dome, the points of the crescent aimed toward the earth and the arch pointed to the heavens. The church had two wooden doors in the front, covered with gold etching—both closed.

A beggar with twinkling eyes in shrunken sockets leaned against the doors, a crumpled fedora perched on his head. A small crowd had gathered in front of the church, some on their knees, more of them up and chatting.

Clye kept his head down and shuffled up to the beggar. The little man showed a gap-toothed grin and removed his hat.

"Howdy," he said.

"Howdy," Clye returned, disgust slipping into his tone. "I see you got the hat, *kive*."

"Wasn't easy," the beggar smiled, pulling the hat to his chest and extending his free hand.

Clye nodded, opening his jacket and pulling out his short sword.

The beggar's eyes shone as Clye put the sword in his hands. The beggar looked the sword up and down a moment before drawing it to his chest. He handed the hat to Clye, who nodded.

"Now get outta here," Clye said, "before the Law catches you peddling on a holy day."

"Glory be to the Sandwalker," the beggar said, rushing to his feet and scampering away.

Clye tried to smooth the dents and clear the cobwebs off of the gray fedora. Oh well. It was a hat, a blacksmith's fedora no less. Same sort of hat Clye lost in a bar fight a month ago. Clye placed it on his head, twisting it back and forth till it settled comfortably. He smiled. *Upstanding citizen.*

Clye backed away from the doors and knelt on the sand with a few of the other men. Better not to attract attention.

A coughing fit took him, and Clye had to pound his chest to calm his lungs. Clye didn't look up to see if the crowd had stared.

The praying of townsfolk resumed around him. They sent prayers up to the Sandfields of the Sun, where the Sandwalker now lived. Clye kept his eyes on the sand beneath his knees and hoped he wouldn't end up in Hona for his lack of piety. Kein, he was already going to Hona; unless he redeemed his name. That might save his sullied soul.

A quarter of an hour later, a minister pushed the doors open, his white turban bright in the sunlight. His white suit and gold tie and belt were equally luminous.

"Welcome, citizens of Jute, to the holy church," he called out over the crowd, smiling. "Let us worship the glory of the Sandwalker today."

"Glory be to the Sandwalker!" the crowd chanted. Clye missed the cue but was able to mouth the last couple syllables.

The minister nodded to the crowd, turned on his heels, and vanished into the church.

Bit by bit, the crowd followed—well-dressed individuals first, poorer folks after. Clye slipped in last.

Sunlight filtered into the church through a few high windows cut in the marble like lashes in the back of a thief. Wooden pews flanked either side of the central aisle, and at the far end, a marble dais rose out of the floor. Beneath the arch, the minister stood like a mountain tree growing out of the stone.

Clye snuck into one of the back pews, empty except for a short man in a bowler hat. As Clye sat down, realization dawned on him, and he froze.

But it was too late to get up. The minister was calling out "Please stand as we sing the 'Ballad of the First Mountain Moving'."

As everyone stood, Clye pulled his hat down over his eyes and hoped Shorty wouldn't recognize him. The minister raised his hand and started singing.

*"O Great Sandwalker on high,*
*We sing to Thee of ancient day,*
*When mountain Thou movedst,*
*And stone Thou brokest,*
*And moved the weight of Law*
*To freedom grant to thirsty souls,*
*Who come to Thee guilty,*
*Receiving cleansing,*
*But even so die*
*Like dogs or saints*
*At our own hands…"*

Clye didn't know a single word of the song, but he followed along as best he could, stealing glances at the man beside him. Under the bowler, the little fellow had long sideburns and pristine fingernails. The way his chin jiggled as he sang reminded Clye of a pig the Yeller gang kept. It was short and black with tiny hooves and massive jowls. Good pork that one turned out to be.

When the ballad came to a close, the minister waved his hands and announced the next song. They probably sang four hymns in all—Clye forgot to keep track. It was strange, all these dusty people of all classes singing together, most of them off-key. And why? Why a song? And if they were singing to the Sandwalker, was he supposed to respond with a chorus of his own? Or come down and absorb their praises?

And yet, something felt very *right* about the whole affair. Clye couldn't put his finger on it. He might've enjoyed the hymns if it weren't for the little man beside him. They'd almost had a shootout.

The minister interrupted Clye's thoughts. "Please, people of Jute, be seated as we hear a reading from the holy Annals of the Sandwalker."

Everyone sat down in unison, Clye again, late on the cue. He stole a glance at Shorty. The little man wore a wide grin, the smell of smoke wafting off of him as he situated on the pew.

Up on the dais, the minister now hefted a massive leather book in his arms, pages spilling out like bird's wings on either side of him.

"*Kone iv'ain shote fallaw, iv'aallow. Noske iv'ollin, shote drani odh iv'Drode...*" the minister droned, each syllable drawling out of the side of his clean-shaven mouth.

Clye felt a jab in his side. He turned.

22

The man in the bowler grinned at him, leaned in and whispered, "I like your hat, kid. Blacksmith...or bounty hunter?"

Clye glanced back up at the minister, who was still reading loudly. He pivoted back to the little man. "What do you want?" he whispered.

The little man smiled. Gold glinted in the recesses of his mouth. He extended his hand, said, "Hollin Wesner, casino giant. I need a bartender, kid—hard man like you. My current one can't tell the difference between valagu and brandy—drinks plenty of both, though. Eh? What do ya say? Pays well."

Clye's pulse rose. A job was what he wanted—*needed*. A job meant respect—a place for a name to attach itself and grow in safety and status.

"Yes," he said. He shook Hollin's hand before a second thought could enter his head.

Hollin smiled. "After the reading and interpretation I'll show you around the saloon." His smile faded. "But don't sleep by it again—I'll have you arrested. Bad for business. Very bad. Let's not have a repeat of this morning, eh?"

Clye nodded, felt Hollin's little hand slip from his as he turned and watched the minister again.

Job. He now had a job—not a cowboy, but...a job still. *If only Pa were here.*

THE SALOON WAS a massive building—very wide and two stories tall. Brick pillars made up the building's corners and lined the doorways and windows. The rest was sided with various grades of wood. The wooden shingles on the roof appeared to have been replaced many times—thought over, fretted over, replaced with the same material—only a little less sun-worn. But no matter how many times they were replaced, eventually, the cycle would begin again. The shingles would die—crack under the hot sun or peel off in the wind.

Well-used steps led up to a pair of batwing doors.

Hollin trotted up the stairs and shoved his way through the doors. They swung loosely behind him. Clye slipped in quietly.

"Nice saloon, eh?" Hollin said.

Clye glanced about the room. Chair-ringed tables cluttered the place from the right side of the room almost all the way to the left, where a large counter stood draped in an exotic skin rug. Bottles decorated the wall behind the counter. The usual wooden divider went from the right wall to six feet short of the counter—to keep the drunks from the families.

"Ain't bad," Clye said.

"Eh, could be better." Hollin waved a hand. "But she was cheap. She's my second saloon, you know? You wanna see the back? Part of your job," he chuckled.

Hollin trotted up to the counter. He ran his hand along it, short fingers bobbing as they crossed the thick, billowing fur stretching across the countertop. The fur was a warm, golden brown, very thick, mottled with fine white hairs.

"Angoraeth fur," he said quietly. "Lives far south of here— you know they have ice down there? Beasts lay hundreds of eggs through their lives, protect 'em, gather 'em up before hatching them the day they die." Hollin looked up at Clye, wrinkles pinching the skin around his eyes. "Sad they have to die before they see the profit, eh? Well."

He tapped the counter and moved on.

A door stood in the far corner. Hollin pulled a key from his sleeve, unlocked it, pushed his way in. Clye followed.

The back room contained three cast iron stoves, all positioned against the left-hand wall. A long counter ran parallel in the center of the room. Sacks and barrels were stacked against the far wall like stones over a grave. In the right corner rose a narrow stairway that disappeared up into the ceiling.

Hollin pointed at the stoves. "The cooks work down here— all you'll have to do is yell at them. Up there—" he pointed up the stairs—"is my office. You'll run up there to get your pay every Sixth Day." His brow furrowed. "That's the only time you go up there, you hear? Not any other day but Sixth Day."

Clye straightened, nodded. "Of course."

"Well, then," Hollin rubbed his hands together, "This'll be fun, kid. Say, I should probably ask, you ever been a bartender before?"

"No, sir. But I've watched enough of 'em to know the basics."

"Ah, well, I see." Hollin scratched at his sideburns. He squinted up at Clye. "I'm going to guess you were an outlaw once, is that right?"

"Why do you say that?" Clye dropped one hand to his hip, glanced back at the door. He could suddenly feel the scars on his forefinger.

Hollin held up a hand. "Wait," he said. "What men are most familiar with saloons, eh? Town drunks, yes, bounty hunters, of course, and outlaws. You're not a town drunk—I know every regular and you're not any of 'em. You're obviously not a bounty hunter as we proved this morning."

He smiled. "So you're an outlaw. Now don't get alarmed, I like hard men. We all have a past, don't we?"

Hollin peered over at the stoves as if they were listening, then looked up at Clye.

"I'm not a popular man, Mr. Outlaw," he whispered. "I own saloons and casinos and the church has lots of nasty things to say about such places, *but...*" He shook his head. "Let me give you a tip. You can't run from your past, Mr. Outlaw. Have to embrace it. That's where you find inner peace."

Hollin flashed a smile, but it didn't quite reach his eyes.

Clye released his pistol grip and nodded to the casino giant. Every time he thought about going back to outlawry, it sounded like hona to him—always killing, always running. Even now, years away from outlawry, he had no inner peace. Peace was something Clye Galler had only had when he was young and short and played all day with his bald father.

"Now, ready to mix a few drinks, my friend?"

Clye snapped from his stupor and looked down at the little man in the bowler hat. "Yeah. Course I am." But his voice lacked enthusiasm. Clye's thoughts danced around his head like his father bucking around the house like an imbval.

## FOUR
# I WANT YOU

THE SALOON was bustling that first night—the evening of First Day, as no saloon was open on a holy day. Hollin stuck around for the first hour of it, giving Clye pointers and letting him know the orders of a few regulars. Then he vanished into his office, leaving Clye in the charge of the previous bartender—an old lady who claimed she'd never had a taste of liquor in her "whole livin' born days."

The sun had fallen in the west, most of the women and children had left, and the saloon was illuminated by greasy oil lamps swinging from the rafters. They cast a warm glow over the room, bordered by tendrils of darkness that leapt up when the wind gushed in through a window.

Clye walked into the kitchen, a bowler hat from Hollin placed firmly on his head. He strode up to the long counter where a few of the flour-stained cooks were working. One of them—a middle-aged woman in a blue dress—glanced up, rolled her eyes, and handed Clye a steak on a plate.

"Who's this for?" Clye asked.

The lady shrugged her shoulders so fast that flour billowed

off her dress. "You took the order, you should remember."

Clye bowed, swore, and carried the plate out into the main room. He glanced at the "drunk" side of the room, scanning the faces, trying to remember whose order it was that he held in his hand. Most of the tables were ringed with three or four men playing cards. One man, however, sat alone, his wide-brimmed bounty hunter's hat pulled down low over his eyes. A little pile of sand sat on the table—probably scooped up from the floor. The man periodically pinched a bit and tossed it in his mouth. Clye remembered him from earlier that night—possibly the man who ordered the steak. For a moment Clye almost thought—but no. They were all dead. Except Justin, maybe.

Inhaling, Clye strode up to the round table and addressed the bounty hunter. He forced his voice to sound polite. "Sir, you order a nawfa steak—no onions?"

The man tipped the brim of his hat—a nod?

Clye quickly set the iron plate down on the table. The clunk echoed, but not loud enough that it disturbed the hum of chatter and laughter in the room. The man looked at the plate.

"I didn't order a steak," he said, and hiccupped. "Didn't order a steak, bartender."

"Sorry, sir," returned Clye, and picked up the plate.

"Hey!" The man reached up and grabbed Clye's arm with his pale, scarred hand—three deep cuts on the index finger. "My name's not 'sir,' bartender—it's Ross."

Clye yanked his arm away, almost flinging the steak off the plate.

Ross's arm thunked down on the table. He tipped his head so Clye could see his face—young, barely an adult, but wrinkled and weathered. His pupils were massive, eyelids half-closed. "Mind bringin' over a drink, bartender?" he drawled, leaning down over the table, putting his cheek to the wood. He snorted in a breath, inhaling most of the pile of sand that lay there.

"If you pay for it," Clye said, his mind far away from his words. He'd seen the three scars. *There was no Ross in the Yeller gang.* Then again, neither was there a Clye.

"I can pay, sure," Ross reached into his vest pocket and pulled out a few copper kaj.

"What do you want?"

Ross smiled, but his eyebrows were narrowed. He pushed his hat up, reached in and pulled out a folded and sealed paper. He clamped the hat back down and placed the paper on the table, shoved it forward with two fingers—first and third.

"I want *you*, Lyle Yeller," he said, smile vanishing.

Clye froze, knuckles whitening as he gripped the iron plate. He saw the two fingers, first and third: a bounty being issued.

Clye stepped forward to the bounty hunter and leaned in. "I'm sorry, Mr. Ross, but there is no Yeller gang anymore. I don't know how you got me mixed up with one of them but I'd advise you to move on. Good day—"

Ross gripped Clye's dark forearm again, staring up at him with his wide eyes. "I know who you are, Lyle Yeller. I was a Yeller myself, yeah? My name was Filone Yeller, you remember?"

Clye bit his lip. He did. He remembered that kid—bad limp and a worse heart.

Ross's smile grew wider. "I see you do. You love me—my name, yes? You still love me, no?"

Clye wrinkled his nose. "What the kein are you talking about?"

Ross frowned. "No…no…you hate me." His nostrils flared, head bobbed to the side. "Request of Justin Croy, I compel you to engage me in a duel to the death, *Lyle Yeller*."

Clye swung the plate and struck him across the forehead. Ross screamed and let go of Clye's arm. Clye rushed back to the counter where the old lady was having her first ever swig of moonshine. He glanced back at the tables. Ross had risen, hand to his forehead, blood and steak drippings smeared all over it. Some of the other men had turned around and were shouting. They sounded very far away.

Clye had struck a man—the blow would've killed Ross if he'd hit harder. He hadn't done that in so long, so many years. He'd thought he was over it—a better man.

*Well.* He gripped his pistol.

Ross stopped, one hand on his own hip, eyebrows furrowed but pupils still dilated.

The crowd had backed away, some of them calling for the idiots to take the duel outside, others settling at seats in the back, placing bets.

Ross looked down at the sand and dust on the floor, closed his eyes.

*Kein.*

The dust on the ground vibrated, each particle bouncing madly off the ground. One of the regulars yelled something—"Take it outside!" or something of the sort. Clye backed up against the counter and felt the angoraeth fur against his back.

Clye could hear the old lady's raspy voice behind the counter. "Sand-duel? Take the children out immediately!" But there were no children left in the saloon.

The sand began to swirl into a large flurry revolving around Ross. Ross's eyes remained closed, one hand on his forehead, one hand on his pistol. The sand spiraled faster and faster, thicker and thicker. It swirled into a whirlwind, taking up a quarter of the room. People in the back ducked, shouted in protest.

The sand engulfed Clye in seconds. He coughed, heard one or two others coughing. He tried to keep his eyes open but the sand burned them. He drew his pistol and shot blindly into the whirlwind.

Someone screamed—not in pain, Clye knew that sound too well. A scream of anger. A gunshot followed, striking the counter next to him. The old lady shrieked in Clye's ear. Clye held his gun up, tried to see Ross and couldn't. He fired again. A grunt. He holstered.

The sand slowed, someone was shouting "The Law! The Law! Indoor sand duel!" at the top of their lungs.

Clye felt fewer particles striking his arms. He opened his eyes.

The crowd huddled in the back corner, eyes wide. A few yards from Clye, his back to the crowd, stood Ross—pistol raised, right arm tucked against his side. Blood stained his sleeve. Ross's eyes were bright as sparks off a house fire, deadly as a snake's.

Clye lunged at Ross. Ross fired, but missed. Clye barreled the younger man over, knocking down the table. A few regulars scrambled away, rushing for the door. The old lady wept behind the counter.

Clye gripped Ross's collar, pounded his head against the floorboards. Sand flew up with each strike.

"Enough!" shouted Ross.

Clye stopped, staring at the young but wrinkled face, blood trickling from the forehead wound into his eyes.

"You forfeit your bounty on my life?" Clye hissed.

Ross bit his lip, then slowly nodded.

Clye exhaled. "Good. Now leave me alone. I don't want to see your face ever again...*Yeller.*" And Clye kissed the hunter's eyeball like the Yellers did before expelling a member.

The blood stained his lips. Clye rose to his feet. The crowd had mostly fled, and those who remained looked at the fallen bounty hunter with wide eyes. It was always a sight to witness a bounty hunter and his prey. Even more so to see that prey *best* the hunter—in an indoor sand-duel, no less. The church would be gossiping about this for weeks.

Clye exhaled and ran out of the saloon.

He ran, boots pounding the sand, bowler hat still perched on his head. He wove through the streets, hunting for an alley. Between a shadowed old hotel and a skeletal mansion, Clye found a dark corner where he could hide from the light of the moon. He plopped onto the ground, placing his back to the mansion's pale yellow siding. His breaths came in gasps—it had been a hard run and a hard fight. The blood tasted metallic on his lips. Clye wiped his mouth on his jacket sleeve of the same color.

His chest heaved. *I'm exactly the same,* he thought. *I'm an outlaw.*

Five years since the gang was destroyed, and still those habits were ingrained in him.

Clye put his hand to his forehead. Sweat coated his fingers. *Lyle Yeller, outlaw.* The Law would come, and Ross would tell, and Clye would be hanged for his crimes.

32

Clye rubbed his eyes furiously, clenched and unclenched his fists, ground his teeth together. His chest tightened as he remembered that was how Yellers got ready before a raid.

"I ain't Yeller no more!" he shouted, looking up at the hotel across the alley as if it might answer and confirm for the world that Clye Galler was not an outlaw.

He could skip town—try his luck at a restart in Crayridge or Valkar. A job like a cowboy or a minister would immediately earn him respect. Or Clye could go back to Hollin and ask him to sort things out. He had said he was a "casino giant." Seemed a powerful position—but it was far from Sixth Day.

Clye pulled his pistol out of its holster. He pulled the hammer back halfway, flipped the cylinder out. Three bullets left. With his free hand he reached into the ammo pouch at his belt and gathered three more, pressing each carefully into the cylinder chambers. He closed up the revolver, holstered it, rose to his feet.

He'd skip town. He had to. His name had been blabbed, the whole town would know about the duel—there was nothing else he could do.

Clye walked out of the alley, pulled his hat down over his forehead, and turned up the street—north, toward the jagged mountains ringing the desert like the body of a petrified snake.

A deafening roar split the air and the ground shook. Light flashed in the sky behind the bony remains of the mansion.

Clye steadied himself. He knew a bank heist when he heard one—felt one. The town would be in an uproar—the perfect moment to escape. Or…to prove that he was an upstanding citizen by catching the outlaws before the Law showed up.

Clye shifted his feet, the grains of sand crunching beneath his boots. Inhale. Exhale. Clye spun on his heels and rushed back into the alley he'd come from. The end was blocked by a tall wooden fence. Clye backed up a few paces and bolted toward the fence. He jumped into the air at the last moment, clawing for a handhold as he struck the fence. His right hand snatched the top of one of the posts, and he dragged himself upward till he could get his ribs over the top. Clye surveyed the street beyond. A massive wood-and-stone building flying a golden flag—a bank—stood across from him, its rear wall facing him. The rear wall had been blown apart, some bits of wood on fire. Lamps showed in many windows of houses that lined the street, but the street was yet empty of life.

Clye nodded, clenched his teeth, and heaved himself over the fence. He rolled as he hit the sand below, stirring up a massive cloud. He rose, then stumbled. Clye coughed the sand from his lungs, surprised at how it dried his chest and shot pain into his head. It'd been over two weeks since he'd had a grain—the pain should have lessened by now. Clye shook his head and stood up straight.

Smoke and dust hung in a cloud behind the bank. Clye adjusted his hat, drew his revolver, and rushed from his dusty cloud into that sooty one.

He clambered over the pile of scorched rubble, and hopped into what had been the vault of the bank. It was all shadow here—shapes only discerned by light of the half-pint flames licking broken bits of wood. A tall iron safe stood in a corner, split open and emptied. The racks and drawers had been emptied or strewn over the ash-covered vault floor. A door stood open at the far end of the room. Voices drifted from beyond it.

Clye tiptoed up to the door and peered through.

Ross and five other men stood around the bloodied corpse of a bank guard. Most of them held bulging sacks slung over their shoulders.

"Not sure where the kive went," Ross said to a tall outlaw holding a long sword.

The outlaw swayed slightly while he held the tip of his short-brimmed blacksmith's fedora. "Probably skipped town," he said.

Clye froze. He knew that voice anywhere. Justin Croy, his only friend in the Yeller Gang, and the best with grains out of anyone he'd ever met. They both adored books and apples. Apples most of all.

Clye's hand shook, but he raised his pistol. Both these men knew him. They'd tell. Ross would be easy to kill, but Justin...the man had talent with sand power and sword that few possessed.

Clye slowly stepped into the doorway, a little moonlight shining against his back. He trained his pistol-sight on Ross's head.

Clye spoke in a gruff voice, pitched lower than his own, "Stay where you are."

The outlaws each stiffened, turned toward him. A few of them started to raise their hands, but Ross interrupted.

"Now stop this—stop, all of you. This is Lyle Yeller we're lookin' at."

Each outlaw immediately grabbed his weapon. Clye ducked back into the vault just as a shower of bullets snapped through the air.

"Wait!" The voice of Justin Croy.

A pause. Clye brought his revolver to his chest and locked his eyes on the empty doorway.

*Just try to come through,* he thought.

"Know you're in there, Lyle," Justin called. "I could kill you with a snap of my fingers. Or rip you apart—if you were made of sandstone. Come out. I swear on the bones of the Old Yeller that I won't touch a hair of your head."

"What about your men?" Clye returned. "Will they swear?"

"On the life of Dayer Proyton, they swear," Justin said, his voice low, grave.

*Alright.* Clye struggled to his feet and stepped gingerly into the doorway.

The outlaws still stood around the corpse, each grasping weapons, gripping their sacks.

Justin stepped over the corpse, hand pinching the brim of his hat. He walked a stride or two closer to Clye, sword in hand.

Clye raised his pistol.

Justin stopped, tipped his chin up. Light glinted off his teeth. "How many apples have you stolen?"

Clye didn't move.

Justin nodded. "I won't hurt you. But I will have you know that Dayer Proyton is not someone to be trifled with. You're a good shot, but you insult us." His teeth vanished. "Next time I send a bounty hunter on you, you read the notice and you *follow the rules*. Eh? Can you do that?"

"I ain't dueling a hunter in a saloon—my name—"

"He said it was a duel?" Justin's voice was ice.

"To the death."

Justin turned to Ross, sword in hand. "We'll discuss this later," he said, nodded.

Ross said nothing, just shifted where he stood.

Justin pivoted back to face Clye. "Will you come with us, Lyle? Dayer would *love* to meet you. In fact he's asked for you personally."

"I'd sooner shoot you," Clye said.

"You won't, though."

A sinking feeling settled over Clye's stomach. He couldn't shoot Justin—they'd been too close. It was time, not anger that had separated their friendship.

A gunshot split the air.

Clye ducked, turned around. Two lawmen carrying long rifles were jumping up the rubble toward them.

"Lyle! Lyle Yeller!" cried Justin, leaping forward and grabbing Clye by the arm. "I'll see you soon, my friend," he whispered into his ear, and shoved him.

Clye fell against the sooty floor of the vault, and one of the lawmen was over him.

Shouting, gunshots, a rifle butt being rammed into his head. The world went as black as Clye's outlaw past.

# FIVE

# A LETTER

CLYE'S HEAD THROBBED.

He felt hard stone biting into his cheek, his chest, his knees. Clye put his hand to his temple, feeling the veins bulge with blood. He shook his head, winced as his nose scratched against the stone.

"Kein..." he muttered, lifting his head a little off the ground to rub his nose.

Clye opened his eyes. He lay on his stomach in a stone-floored cell, watching the iron bars rise into the ceiling above him.

Beyond the bars was a wood-paneled room with a desk shoved against the left wall piled with books and papers. A lawman in a white hat sat at the desk, staring at a book while twirling his equally white mustache. His vest and breeches were a smooth, clean brown leather.

Sunlight illuminated the whole place, leaking in through a window beside the skinny front door in the far wall.

Clye lowered his gaze to the floor again. Bits of yellow sand were scattered across the gray stone—flakes of death or power—er. He licked his lips—dry.

Clye pushed himself to his knees. His head swam. Hand to forehead, teeth gritted, he rose to his feet. The floor danced beneath his feet, and Clye rocked to stay standing. A wooden bench squatted by the cell wall. Carefully, Clye sat down on the bench.

He shook his head. *Jailed.* He'd only been in a Law House once before, but that was to break Justin Croy out when the Law caught him seven years ago. Now Clye was the one behind bars. Justin had said he would see him soon, but Clye doubted a jailbreak. No, Justin would visit at the hanging— watch him swing from the crimson rope.

Clye glanced at the lawman. He still stared at his book, twirling his mustache in what appeared to be profound concentration.

The outlaw put his hand to his head. He'd hang for his crimes, and no one would care—except his parents. The outlaw inhaled, surprised at how little air he drew in. He swallowed.

The outlaw had failed. No matter how much good he did, his crimes would always outweigh it. He would always be an outlaw.

The squeak of chair legs against stone.

Clye looked up to see the lawman rising out of his chair, open book in his hand, walking up to the bars of the jail cell. He was a skinny man, with small blue eyes that seemed to know as much as they asked.

"Howdy," said the lawman.

"Howdy," answered the outlaw.

The lawman cleared his throat. "Well, Mr. Yeller, it appears you're wanted in a whole bundle of towns across Drode, includin' Jute. Now, I'm shore a hard man like yourself can take what I'm about to give out. So," he cleared his throat again and squinted down at his book. "Accordin' to the Lawbook of two-two-nineteen, I sentence you, Lyle Yeller, to be hung and drawn within a fortnight of today. I'm sure you know your crimes, but I'll list 'em accordin' to the Lawbook of two-two-nineteen: food theft, bank robbery, rape, unlicensed drinking of water from the Cawlin well, murder, and the stealin' of five fine steeds these ten years ago."

The lawman snapped his book shut, worked his thin jaws in a chewing motion as he eyed the outlaw. "I'm Sheriff T. Quave. We'll be spendin' a lot o' time together these days, Mr. Yeller. Pleasure to meet ya." He tipped his hat, walked back over to his desk.

Clye pursed his lips, looked down at his boots. He could feel that they'd taken the hidden knife out of it. He patted his belt. Empty ammo pouch, empty holster. He felt the inside of his jacket. They'd left the salra, thank the Sandwalker.

He turned his head toward the sheriff who was now writing something with a quill pen.

"Sheriff Quave, may I write home to my ma and pa?"

Quave swiveled in his seat and peered through the bars at Clye. He pursed his mustached lips. "Mail don't go out for another day or two," he said.

Clye shrugged. He fought the tear creeping up in his eyes. "I just wanna tell them that I appreciated them."

Quave held a fist under his chin. "I don't see no harm in that. You'll have to write in Common Drodhi," he picked up a paper and quill pen and walked up to the bars of the cell. "None of that Proyton scratch and outlaw codes." Quave handed the paper and pen through the iron bars, and Clye rose and took them with a nod.

"Thank you, sir," Clye bowed.

Quave sniffed, then shrugged. "Polite for an outlaw," he muttered as he sat back down at his desk.

Clye knelt down on the ground and placed the paper flat on the surface of the wooden bench. He rolled the pen in his fingers a moment, eyes on the blank sheet. What would he say? "Pay the price on my head"? No, that was several thousand *bokaj*—his parents had never been that wealthy.

Clye bit his lip—bit it until he tasted blood. He'd seen enough hangings to imagine what it felt like—the humiliating hat-burning, the hanging itself, the sword that sliced the abdomen of those who'd committed more serious crimes: murder, steed-theft, rape, church-burning. He'd never burnt a church, but he'd done the others several times over. He wondered which of the four the dangling outlaw in the square had done.

Kein, he thought he could redeem himself! It was easy for family to love each other—they shared blood and name. Doing good deeds in the sight of church—getting a job, helping widows and beggars as Clye often did—would be enough to win the love of a town...unless you were an outlaw. Could a respectable job have redeemed the bloodstained name of Lyle Yeller? If it could, it was too late now.

Lyle Yeller was an outlaw—worthless scum of Drode. Now he would die. Good riddance.

Clye put the pen to paper, scratching the words down as they came in his head.

> *Dear Ma and Pa,*
>
> *I'm to be hanged. I love you both so dearly. I'm ashamed I haven't been the good son you'd hoped*

*to raise. If you can help me, I beg you to, but I know the price on my head is far too high for you to pay. I pray the Sandwalker that you visit me in the prison of Jute, three and a quarter days by foot from Annaday.*

*Please Ma. Please Pa.*

*Visit me. I do not deserve your love, but I return it with this letter, as much as an outlaw can.*

*With deepest regret and love,*
*Clye Galler*

Clye folded up the paper, kissed it, and rose.

FOUR DAYS PASSED. Sheriff Quave would squeeze a morsel of bread and a tin cup of water through the bars every morning, and a bruised apple through them every night. Clye loved the apple.

It was nice to have this regularity after five years of wandering Drode without a home. The five years of gang life, while regimented, had been unpredictable. You never knew when the white-bearded Old Yeller would burst into a fit of rage and shoot someone.

Clye sipped from his cup. The coolness eased his dry throat. "Those were the days," he muttered.

The Old Yeller had never killed a member of the gang—they were too small for that. But the faded gun-wound still throbbed in Clye's side.

The door of the Law House creaked open. Clye looked up to see a lean man stride in, skin as dark as Clye's own, neck slouched forward beneath a wide-brimmed hat. The man had a handsome face, but there was something dark about him—something that turned Clye's stomach. Perhaps it was the bloodstained rifle slung over his shoulder.

Quave rose, his spurs clacking against the floor, and the stranger tipped his hat to him.

"You find 'em?" Quave said.

The stranger shook his head. "No prints to track. We guess that they fled to the mountains."

"Kein!" Quave kicked at the stone floor. "Keinin' outlaws done slipped us again!"

The stranger nodded, glance flitting to Clye for a moment. "Proyton is clever. They have Justin Croy with them—I heard once that he lifted a three-ton boulder with sand power, once created a storm that engulfed an entire bank. He's better with sand power than anyone I've ever seen, and I've—"

"'Traveled Drode over—every dune I've seen and every rock I've prodded.' I know, Jenaven, I *know*." Quave twirled his mustache. "Hmm. Leave me be for a few days. I'll come up with somethin'," he said.

Jenaven stood still a moment. "I killed Sheriff Verrod Rass for you."

The coolness with which he said it worked shivers down Clye's spine. *Bounty hunters.*

"'Bout time." Sheriff Quave strode over to his desk, picked up a folded piece of paper. He started handing it to Jenaven, then hesitated. "How do I know you offed him?"

Jenaven motioned to the door. "The body's outside. Payment?" He held his hand out.

Quave wrinkled his nose, then handed the paper over. "Well, can't say you're unstained, but you're the best in the business.

And you got respect, for a son of Bu'rone. Never failed to bring back a corpse."

Jenaven nodded, turned on his heels, and pushed his way out the door, sunlight flashing in before the door shut—like a final kiss before the noose went taught.

Quave turned and faced his desk, scratching his chin. The shadow from his hat concealed his face. "Least we got one outlaw," he muttered.

Clye took another sip of water, but his throat felt constricted. He felt the slight tickle in his lungs—a calling for grains. Clye burst out coughing, spat out what water remained in his mouth. He pounded his chest, swearing under his breath. Quave didn't seem to notice.

The sheriff had just begun to sit down at his desk when someone knocked on the door from outside. He pounded his fist against the desk.

"Come in!" he snapped.

A skinny postman in a gray cap stepped into the door, a bulging satchel slung at his side. He fished a stack of envelopes out of it, stepped across the wooden floor to the sheriff.

"Mail, Sheriff," the postman said, handing Quave the letters.

"Thank 'ee," Quave growled, snatching them. He flipped through the envelopes. "Safe trip?"

"Mostly, sir. Cardan had to fend off a couple o' bandits when we left Rossler but they didn't give us much trouble."

"Good," Quave nodded.

The postman bowed, then straightened his cap.

Quave waved him away. "Alrighty. Head off. Sandwalker guard your name."

"Same to you," the postman returned, spinning on his heels

and marching out the door, each footfall echoing against the stone floor.

Quave flipped through the envelopes again, lips pursed.

"Well, Mr. Yeller, looks like we got a letter here for a 'Clye Galler.' That you?"

Clye's heart leaped in his chest. His parents had answered. "Yessir," he said.

Quave nodded, threw the envelope against the far wall. It hit the wood with a flat smack, bounced down to the stone floor. Clye stared. The letter lay far out of reach in the corner of the office, sealed with a big piece of wax red as blood. A small cloud of dust hung in the air around the letter, its only mourner.

Clye looked up at Quave, trying to read the sheriff's face. Quave had settled back into his chair and was opening one of the other envelopes with a small knife. His lips were pursed, his eyes flicked back and forth down the page. The sheriff sighed, let the letter he was holding fall down onto the desk. He turned toward Clye, eyebrows knit, his mouth turned downward in a lazy frown. "Been in prison before, Outlaw?" he drawled.

Clye scratched his head, grateful they let him keep the bowler hat. Clye paused, brushing the felt with his fingertips. "I'm not an outlaw," he said, a tremor slipping into his voice.

Quave smiled. "Don't sound like you believe it."

Clye licked his dry lips. It felt like the walls around him were closing in, ready to choke the very life out of him. It was as if the bone-dry floor and the dead oak walls had grown hands and minds and voices that rasped "You are an outlaw. You are *stained*."

Clye let out a sigh—long, dusty, heavy. He blinked, found

tears in his eyes. His gaze fluttered to the letter lying alone in the corner. Words formed in his head—*If only I'd never left home. If only I'd been the son my parents deserved. If only I could get a job. If only I could redeem my hona-keined blood-stained name!*

Clye looked up at Quave, who had begun scratching something on a paper with his quill pen.

"Sheriff?"

A groan that cast a shadow over the prison. Quave turned to Clye. "What's on your mind, Outlaw?"

"What would you feel if you knew you were to be hanged in a week and four days?"

Quave pursed his lips. "Hmm." Twirled his mustache. "Hmm. I suppose I'd be right terrified, son. Right terrified."

"What if you knew that no one in the world cared if you were hung?"

Quave scratched his chin, shook his head slowly. "I don't know, son," he said, "that's a sorry plight, right here. But lemme tell ya somethin', there are plenty of right sorry plights in this world—yours *veritably* ain't the only."

He turned back to his desk.

Clye sighed, realized he was still holding the empty tin cup. He set it on the sand-strewn floor beneath his feet and straightened so his spine popped. A week and three days. Ten days. Ten days and Drode would be rid of that notorious outlaw, Lyle Yeller.

He'd imagined his hanging so many times, never knew that this was what it felt like to be so near it—a surreal resignation and calm, mixed with an agonizing fear, and torture knowing what would come. Alone, very alone, except for a sheriff that was no comfort at all. Clye put his head in his hands and closed his eyes. If only he could've outweighed the evil in his life with good.

Slowly, he opened his eyes. In the corner the lone letter still sat, the red wax looking more and more like blood from the mouth of an outlaw hanged but minutes ago.

He'd tried to redeem himself. His parents had tried to help. But it was over now. He was filth—outlaw to the bone for now and ever.

The outlaw buried his face in his hands and wept.

# SIX

# THIS IS CHARITY WORK

CREAK.

Was that the lazy creak of a rope bearing the burden of a sinful man?

*Scrape.*

Was that the scrape of the executioner's sword against the grindstone?

*Thunk.*

Was that the thunk of the stone pillar dropping down into its hole, abandoning forever the feet that it supported but a moment before?

Clye groaned, the bench beneath him biting into his side. His eyelids flickered before they finally opened. Light shone in through the window beside the skinny door in the far wall. Sheriff Quave had pulled up the front of his chair to the bars of the cell, and he sat in it with trembling fingers. Jenaven stood just beside him, his still-bloody rifle tucked under his arm. He seemed to eye Clye with an air of disdain—nothing unusual, but coming from a killer, it made Clye's chest heat up with anger.

Clye rubbed the sleep from his eyes. He pushed himself up from the bench, managed to get into a sitting position. He inhaled sharply, exhaled, turned toward the sheriff and bounty hunter.

"Howdy," he murmured.

"Howdy," Sheriff Quave nodded, eyes on the floor. His lips were puckered, making his mustache stand out the more. He drummed his fingers on the knees of his clean leather breeches. After a moment, the sheriff narrowed his blue eyes at Clye.

"Mr. Yeller, as things are…" Quave scratched his chin. "Well, here's the deal. You bring in Justin Croy, and we'll clear your name."

Clye's pulse quickened. *Clear my name…* But this was a trap. He'd been the only outlaw they'd managed to catch when the others escaped. They weren't about to give up their prey so easily.

"Very generous thing to offer an outlaw," Clye said.

Jenaven spoke up. "I've heard the stories—you're a better fighter than most if they're true. And you know Justin Croy—he certainly knows you. You know the outlaw way. You will track his scent. Absorb his wrath."

Clye felt anger bubble in his chest. *Absorb his wrath—that's because you've never felt the pain of punishment.* "Why can't you catch him? You kill for a living."

Jenaven rubbed his rifle's trigger guard with his finger. "I don't have an outlaw's stench—the filth that sticks them all together."

"Filth?" Clye clenched his fists. "As if you ain't a murderer."

Jenaven narrowed his eyes. "I live by a code—abide by the law. It is legal. A bounty hunter can kill, an outlaw cannot."

"So the law is unjust." Clye's words were ice.

Jenaven said nothing.

"We got business to attend to." The sheriff cleared his throat, turned to Clye. "Jute's in a sorry plight, Mr. Yeller," he said. "The Proyton Gang has been raidin' us for months—blow up a bank here, church there, steal a whole herd o' naw-fa over there. You see, ain't many men in town who'll risk a neck to go after Proyton—certain death they say." Quave inhaled. "That's our plight—right sorry. Do you understand sorry plights, Mr. Yeller?"

Clye felt his heart sink into his stomach. *It's a trick*, he told himself. Just the thing Quave would pull. His memory flitted back to the letter sitting downcast in the corner. But arresting Justin Croy would make Clye a hero in Jute. He'd move beyond his past and redeem his name.

Clye looked at the sheriff. "How do I know this ain't a trap? How do I know you won't hang me *and* Justin when I catch him?"

Quave shook his head, hands on the worn knees of his breeches. He fixed his eyes on Clye. "Mr. Yeller, it ain't often that I'd put the safety of my town in the hands of an outlaw. I *know* that you can succeed where my best hunter failed. Call it a feelin', call it logic, call it prophecy—" Quave stopped and twirled his mustache, lips pursed, eyes squinted. "Whatever the hona it is, I think I'm lookin' at the man who'll bring an end to Justin Croy and the Proyton Gang. *I* would never hang that man, on my honor. What do ya say, Mr. Yeller?"

Clye inhaled a shaky breath, exhaled it. This wouldn't work. Too risky. Surely a trap. He looked up at the sheriff—an old man at the end of his rope, it seemed. Downcast blue eyes, massive pursed lips, wrinkled sallow skin.

"When do we start?" he said.

Quave smiled. Jenaven stood stoic as Quave rose and pulled a key from his belt. He fitted it into the lock on the cell door and turned it, making a scraping sound.

Clye jumped to his feet, adjusted the hat on his head.

Quave slid the door open, and held out a hand to Clye. Clye shook his hand, but Quave's grip was like a vice. Clye frowned at the pale lawman, who looked up at Jenaven.

"Seal it in blood," Quave said, fingers curled tight and thumb pressing into the little bones on the back of Clye's hand.

Jenaven pulled a knife from his fur-lined leather jacket and stepped forward.

Clye grit his teeth. He tried to pull away. Last time he'd sealed a word in blood was when he took the Yeller's Oath at fourteen.

Jenaven ran his knife over both of their thumbs, letting blood ooze down over their hands. Clye inhaled sharply from the pain, glared at Quave.

"Good," Quave smiled, but didn't let go.

He backed up, dragging Clye out of the cell, bumping into the chair he'd pulled up earlier.

"What are you doing?" Clye hissed, "I thought we had a deal."

"We do, Mr. Yeller, we do," said Quave. "But I cain't just let an outlaw roam wild and free, though, you understand that? Jenaven will watch over ya—help ya with the preparations."

Quave let go of Clye's hand and Clye clutched it to his chest. Without the pressure on it, it seemed to swell three times the size.

Clye glanced at the letter sitting forlorn in the corner by the door. Before he could reach for it, Jenaven stepped over and grabbed his arm. Clye tensed, glared up at the bounty hunter.

Jenaven wore a half-smirk, looked at Clye out of the corner of his eye.

"Let's round up a posse," Jenaven said.

JENAVEN DRAGGED CLYE out of the Law House, his grip tightening with every step. A breeze kicked up the sand in the square—blew it at the two murderers; one legal, one illegal. Clye shut his eyes against the sand, accidentally inhaling some. His lungs swelled and tickled. He coughed, doubling over, but when he rose again he felt taller. When he opened his eyes, Clye could've sworn he could see clearer. That was grains—death through the feet, power through the nose.

Jenaven led Clye across the square. The rotten outlaw corpse still hung from the stone gallows, red rope tight around its neck.

They traveled down the market street, Jenaven bought some fried bavar and two mugs of ale. Clye convinced the bounty hunter to let go of his arm. "You think I'd run away? I'd get shot or hanged. Jenaven, I ain't that stupid."

They sat down on the sand in the shade of the hat shop to eat their food. The beggar who won Clye's sword was nowhere in sight.

"What were you?" Jenaven asked abruptly while they ate.

Clye frowned as he chewed the spongy bavar. "What do you mean?"

Jenaven took a sip of his ale, swallowed loudly, and set his mug down on the sand. "Before," he said. "What were you before you were an outlaw?"

Clye studied the tall hunter. Thin face, nose with a slight beak-like droop, rich brown skin like his, blue eyes with the haughty twinkle of an igru's. Jenaven held his bloody rifle across the knees of his breeches made of yellowed hide. Beneath his jacket he wore a once-white shirt covered with dirt and blood. The blood on both his shirt and his gun seemed intentional—as if the man was making a statement to the world.

"Well?" Jenaven smiled, eyes half-open.

Clye shook his head. "I wasn't anything—I was a kid."

"Crib Outlaw," Jenaven nodded. He grabbed a round bavar from off of the ground and popped it into his mouth. The sand that was stuck to it crunched as he chewed it. "The old posse will not go out again," Jenaven said, turning back to Clye. "We'll have to find new people—hunters would be best, but we need money for that, and I doubt you've got any."

"No, sir," returned Clye. "But I'm sure *you* have plenty to spare."

Jenaven's eyebrows arched down over his eyes. "The business isn't as easy as you kives think," he said. "If you have to know, I've barely gotten ahead. I have some to spare, yes, but not enough to hire six hunters. And even if I did, the price on Justin Croy's head isn't enough to leave a profit after being split eight ways at guild rates."

Clye smirked. "Don't you care about your town? This is charity work."

"Shut your mouth, Outlaw!" Jenaven snapped. "Hona, I hate your kind," he muttered.

"We're both sons of Bu'rone," Clye returned, raising his forearm. "And we're both murderers. We're the same—"

"I am a bounty hunter, *Outlaw.*" Jenaven spit in Clye's face.

Clye snapped his mouth shut, anger roiling within him. His hand shot to his hip, came up empty. He opened his eyes, picked up his mug of ale from the ground, downed it in one gulp. Jenaven glared back at him, one hand resting on the rifle cradled on his knees.

"I've been lookin' for you, Mr. Outlaw," said a voice.

Clye shot to his feet, turned toward the speaker. Hollin Wesner stood in the street, broad smile on his little face, bowler hat perched crooked on his head.

"What do you want, Mr. Wesner?"

Hollin adjusted the lapels of his gray suit. "You know I heard there was an incident a week or so ago? The Law took you in and now all of Jute knows that Hollin Wesner hired *Lyle Yeller* as bartender." His smile vanished. "Those things aren't supposed to get out, Mr. Outlaw."

Clye glanced back at Jenaven, who sat with his rifle still cradled on his knees. The hunter shrugged.

Clye's gaze returned to Hollin. "The Law hired me to catch Justin Croy," he said, "so I can't do anything for your name, Mr. Wesner." A smile flickered at the corners of Clye's lips. "You see, it's *my* name I'm redeeming. If I catch Justin, I'll have earned respect with the world—inner peace, as you'd say."

Hollin's fists clenched, unclenched. Then he smiled. "Justin Croy, eh? I like it. The bounty on his head is enough to buy the DaKobe saloon two times over. I'll join your posse for a third."

Jenaven leaped to his feet. "Not so fast, Wesner. The bounty won't be divided until Justin Croy is imprisoned. We need warriors, not gamblers, in our posse."

"I see." Hollin narrowed his eyes. "I'll hire three bounty hunters to add to your posse—I'll pay them entirely out of my own pocket."

He extended a hand to Clye.

Clye shook Hollin's hand. Three bounty hunters. Wasn't six, but it was enough to get them started.

Clye pulled his hand away.

Hollin smiled, tipped his hat. "I'll put in a reservation for the whole posse at the K'maek Hotel for the night. You two find some steeds for us to set out on tomorrow."

"Will do," Clye said.

Hollin nodded, looked Jenaven up and down. "Now what's your name, my friend? I didn't quite catch it before, you know."

The hunter frowned. "Jenaven Hoyhaiar," he said.

"Mmhm. Too long. I'll call you Hoyhai."

Jenaven cocked the lever on his rifle. "You will not."

Hollin shrugged. "Alright, Jen," he said, turning on his heels and walking away up the street.

Clye chuckled. "Jen. Good name."

Jenaven shook his head. "I hate you."

Clye nodded, chewed on his lip. "Everyone does. Let's find some steeds."

Jenaven tucked his rifle into his armpit and exhaled. "I know a gal who rents steeds by the week. We'll find her stalls at the end of this road. Come on."

He strode forward, kicking up the dust behind him.

A FEW LITTLE cottages lined the market street near its end where it dumped into the vast Drode desert. Many of the cottages had short white fences around them, which enclosed yards of patchy, wilted grass. *Nothin' like Ma's grass,* Clye thought, a smile creeping onto the edges of his lips, while a sinking feeling drew on his heart.

On one of the fences with peeling paint, a curly-headed boy had set up a coin. The boy looked about thirteen, with dark skin and dusty breeches. He wore a black leather jacket. The boy backed up across his yard, brown eyes locked on the coin. Clye stopped, eyed him. The boy pulled a sleek revolver from his pocket and fired. The coin fell to the ground in pieces.

"Nice shot there," Clye said, walking up to the fence.

"We're renting steeds," Jenaven called from the street.

"Just give me a second—I'm talkin' to the kid," Clye returned.

Jen shook his head and walked over to the fence as well.

The boy had holstered his revolver and crossed his arms. He nodded to Clye. "Thank ye," he said, his voice enveloped in a thick brogue.

"What's your name, son?" Clye asked.

"Kobe," said the boy. "Oi'm a moiner."

"Where's your hat?" Jen adjusted his own.

"Moinin' hats're for the moine," Kobe returned. "Ain't no good for shade."

Clye smiled. He liked this kid—reminded him of himself at that age. Bold, crack-shot, logical, defiant. A pang of sadness sank into his chest. Outlawry had seemed so free—so adventurous to his fourteen-year-old heart. "What will you be when you grow up?"

Kobe dusted the sleeve of his black leather jacket. "Ranger," he said. "Or somethin' excoitin'." Kobe shrugged. "Oi don't know." He fiddled with the collar of his jacket. "Oi should probably get back insoide now."

"Why?" Clye said, "Does your mother not let you play?"

"No!" Kobe shook his head adamantly, straightening. "No, she's a good mother, she is. She's moine. Oi—*moiself*, take care o' her. She do the cookin', oi do the workin'.'"

Jenaven grinned. "Strong little man, eh?"

Clye wrinkled his brow, pursed his lips. He put a hand on the fence and looked down at Kobe. "Your mother let you out much?"

The fire left Kobe's eyes. "Oi take the coach to the moine every week—there at the beginnin', back at the end. Moighty far, the moine is."

"What mine is it?"

"Coiter Moine—base of Mount Shonwick," Kobe returned.

Clye nodded. "Ever get days off?"

Kobe kicked at the grass. "Whenever oi need 'em. But days off don't pay, you know."

Clye smoothed the dusty front of his checkered shirt. "How would you like to join our posse and take down Justin Croy? You'll get a share of the reward."

Kobe's eyes grew wide, then he frowned. "How long will it take?"

"Sheriff Quave has given us a week," Jen said. He planted the butt of his rifle in the sand, turned to Clye. "A kid?" he said, not lowering his tone at all. "We need hunters, not children."

"He's a great shot," returned Clye, "and he's a miner. Probably knows the mountains." He turned to Kobe. "Kobe, you know if any gangs live near your mine?"

Kobe looked left and right, though there was no one else around. He turned his eyes up to Clye, nodded.

"See?" Clye said.

Jen shook his head. "I don't like it."

"I don't care what you like. We'll take the kid, get the steeds, bunk in the hotel. Aye?" He winked at Kobe.

Kobe smiled, but his grin fell, turned into a frown. "Oi'll have to ask my mother," he said, glancing back toward the cottage.

"Of course," Clye said.

Kobe pursed his lips, ran up to the porch of the blue-painted house and disappeared inside the door.

"How long will that take?" Jen curled his fists around the barrel of his rifle.

Clye shrugged. "Rent the steeds yourself then," he said.

"I have to keep an eye on you."

"Tie me to this fencepost," Clye returned, scratching his chin. "I don't care. But we're bringin' the kid."

"I don't know." Jenaven eyed Clye, then nodded. He pulled a scarlet cord from within his jacket.

Clye's throat tightened.


AN HOUR PASSED before Kobe came out of the cottage. Clye stood with one hand bound to the fence, the other shoved into the pocket of his breeches. Adventure. Thrill. Those had been the cry of his heart ever since he was a small boy. His parents seldom left the house or did much besides church and gardening. Clye couldn't even recall what his father's job had been.

Clye shook his head, a dry breeze lifting his hat an inch.

Outlaw life had been thrilling. But not how he'd hoped. Robbing banks was fun enough, but killing bankers wasn't. Returning weeks later to the same banks and seeing the bankers' orphaned children begging the streets had torn Clye's heart—ripped his conscience. But he'd been too scared to leave. When the Law found the Yeller's hideout, they killed everyone. Clye could still hear the gunshots, the groans—

could still see the outlaw blood spilled over the desert sand.

But Clye escaped. He thought he was the only one—evidently not. His stomach twisted remembering it took the death of thirteen Yellers to get him to leave outlawry behind.

The cottage door swung open and Kobe hopped out onto the porch. He stood there a moment, back straight, hair tousled. In one hand he gripped a miner's cap. The breeze rustled his jacket, and the boy inhaled deeply. A bright spot shone on his cheek.

"You ready to go?" Clye called.

Kobe exhaled, turned to Clye, jumped off the porch and onto the parched grass. He planted the miner's cap on his head. It was an interesting cap—a metal bowl-shape partly wrapped in leather, with a rough white crystal affixed to the brow. Kobe walked up to Clye.

"Oi'm ready," he said as he took a fleeting glance back at the cottage.

"Good," Clye said. "Jen will be back soon—he'll take us to the hotel for dinner and bed."

Kobe nodded. "Never been to an 'otel."

"I'm sure you'll love it," Clye smiled.

Kobe glanced down at the rope around Clye's wrist. "Y' alright, zurr?"

"Yes." Clye's breathing quickened.

The cord was very red—red as fresh blood flowing from the mouth of a hanged outlaw.

Down the street, the wind blew a cloud of sand high in the air. The grains sprinkled down in a shower, accumulating in a pothole in the middle of the road. The sand nearly filled up the hole. Clye coughed. Sand was good for filling holes. Though not *all* holes, perhaps.

# SEVEN

# THE HEART

EVERY INCH OF the hotel oozed of wealth, of money, and marble gambled off the backs of town drunks. Hollin brought in his three quiet hunters, and the seven-man posse constructed a plan in their shared velvet-carpeted room.

They would go to Coiter Mine and dig Proyton out. Kobe said he'd heard the kives speaking in the walls—most of the miners said it was the wind. Wind or not, it was their only lead and they were taking it.

The next morning, they set out.

The midmorning sun blazed over the market street of Jute, its rays licking every cranny of the stalls without the slightest permission. Vendors grumbled in their booths, their brightly-colored banners snapping above them in the breeze.

Jenaven led the posse through the market, down to the animal stalls that marked the border of Jute and the blistering desert. The stalls were a long row of large wooden huts planted in the sand like so many one-room cottages. Within each stall was enclosed some exotic steed—imbvals, wenkiids, desert melhorns, and others. A picket fence, about chest-high, stood sentry around the stalls, hemming in both the huts and a large spread of sand where various beasts sniffed the dust or pawed the sand with hooves or claws.

Clye smiled as he stepped up to the fence. He'd only ridden a steed once before—when he stole five of them to feed the Yellers—but the thrill stayed with him.

Nearest to him within the enclosure, a cathrahd munched on some sand. It was almost the same color as the sand, with four stumpy legs, the arch of its back about the height of a man raising his arms. The creature was rounded like a ball, armored like a desert dillo but spiny around the sides. It stepped toward Clye, each step grating as the cathrahd dragged its scaly paws forward. The tip of its stumpy tail made a little rut in the sand as it walked. Its massive pointy ears twitched, the comical hog-nose flaring as the creature sniffed this stranger.

Clye thrust his hand between the slats of the fence and clucked his tongue.

The cathrahd squinted at him with its smooth black eyes.

"You like them," Jenaven said, sliding up beside Clye.

The cathrahd snorted and shuffled away.

"I heard that Justin Croy hates animals—is that right?" A smiled played Jen's lips.

Clye shrugged. "None of your business."

"Could come in handy."

Clye pulled his hand back through the fence. "You know what would come in handy?"

Jen tucked his bloody rifle up into his armpit. "What?"

"Weapons. Quave can't expect me to catch Justin Croy with just my two hands—fine weapons though they are."

Jen shrugged. "If I think you need a weapon, I'll hand you one."

"No you won't."

Jenaven said nothing.

Clye grit his teeth. "Who did Quave say would be the man to save Jute? Was it you, the man with the weapons?"

Jen turned to face Clye. He fingered the strap of his rifle. "How much is the life of an outlaw worth?"

Clye's fingers itched to grip a pistol, but his holster was empty. He gripped the crossbar of the fence to steady himself. "I'd say my life is worth an awful lot. Eighty-four thousand—"

"You are worth a rope and a rag to keep your blood from staining the sand." Something sparkled in Jenaven's eyes as he narrowed them. "I doubt they will give you a rag, *Outlaw*."

Clye raised his fists—stopped when Jen's grip tightened on his rifle strap. Slowly, Clye straightened. He extended a hand to Jen.

Jen wrinkled his nose, free hand stuffed into the pocket of his jacket. "What are you doing?"

"I'm glad you're here," Clye smiled. "I'm glad you're fetching our steeds. I'm glad to give you my share of the reward money in return for this *one thing…*" Clye stepped forward and yanked Jenaven's hand out of his pocket, shaking it firmly. "We stick to Quave's agreement. The one I sealed in blood, you remember it? When we get the steeds I'm leading the posse. I'm getting my name cleared. You want the reward, take it! But I'm leading the posse, is that clear?"

He released Jen's hand.

Jenaven straightened, his hat casting a shadow over his face. The glimmer had left his eyes. He turned toward the stalls, cupped a hand to the side of his mouth. "Esta! It's Jenaven! I'm here to pick up the steeds."

"Hang on!" came a distant but harsh female voice.

Clye squinted. A woman appeared on the roof of one of the stall barns, dressed in the garb of a cowboy—wide-brimmed hat with a subtle swoop to it, plaid shirt, leather vest, nawfa-skin breeches and tall boots. She jumped down off of the roof, rolling onto the sand. The cathrahd and other steeds parted for her as she rose. Her hat had fallen off, and as she picked it up, Clye saw her black-and-gray hair pulled back into a bun. Her wrinkled face was even darker than his.

She sauntered up to the fence, reached over and briefly shook Jen's hand. She glanced over at Clye. "Howdy," she said, extending her hand.

"Howdy, ma'am," Clye answered, shaking her hand. Her grip was almost as hard as Sheriff Quave's. When she let go, Clye shoved his hand into his pocket, hiding the scab crossing the width of his thumb—an accessory to the three scars across his first finger.

Esta turned back to Jen and held up her hand. "So you wanted…" she started counting on her fingers, "…three cathrahds and four imbvals, right?"

Jenaven nodded. "Yes, ma'am."

"This is a week-long rental?"

"Yes."

"Good. What are they for?"

Jenaven stiffened, narrowed his eyes. "That is our own business, Esta."

"Really?" she cocked her head and pursed her lips. "You know, I wouldn't like to find that you'd stolen seven good steeds. That's a hangin' crime, that."

Jenaven looked at Clye, a smirk pulling at his lips. Clye straightened, cleared his throat—surprised how tight it felt.

"Ma'am, we've been commissioned by Sheriff Quave to bring in the notorious outlaw Justin Croy. We suspect he's in the mountains, about…" Clye turned around, scanned the posse for Kobe.

"Day and a half by steed," Kobe said, raising his hand.

Clye swiveled back to Esta. "Day and a half out—in Coiter Mine. If you really don't trust us, how 'bout you come out yourself. Save Jute, earn a reward."

"She can't—" Jen started, but Esta cut him off.

"I like that idea," she said. She stood straighter, crossed her arms. "Yeah. I like it. Proyton Gang has no place in Jute." She nodded to Jen. "I'll round up your steeds, leave the stall in good hands, and we'll set out."

Before Jen could say anything, Esta spun on her heels and marched back across the pen, a cloud of dust following behind her.

Jenaven turned to Clye. The look in his eyes said it all. *If you split up the reward again I'll shoot you.*

Clye smiled.


ESTA RETURNED LEADING a train of eight steeds, harnessed and saddled. Jen and the three other bounty hunters each swung onto an imbval—slender, swift antelopes with twisted horns and thick, dappled gray coats.

That left the cathrahds for Hollin, Kobe, Clye, and herself. Esta had to help Kobe and Hollin mount theirs. When Clye got into the saddle, he felt so tall, so powerful, so…free. The breeze whipped at his face, and he was high enough that there was little dust in it. Freedom. Adventure.

"Onward, posse!" Clye shouted, borrowing the words from a book he had read long ago with Justin Croy. The words were childish, but they captured his feeling—the rush of adventure.

The posse behind him gave little grunts or cheers. Jenaven said nothing. Clye nodded.

One didn't need to use spurs on a cathrahd. With the reigns in one hand, Clye slapped the creature's soft neck. It charged forward across the sand, swishing its tail. Clye smiled, looked up at the blue sky with the sun winking down from it.

He would redeem his name. He would earn his place in the world—prove he was worth respect. He could feel it this time. Helping grannies to church or weeding gardens by night had been mere grains on the scale—striving to lift the boulder of sins that held down the opposite pan. But here—this adventure—this would be a stack of bricks to outweigh that boulder, cleanse his spattered name.

The desert stretched flat before them, ground cracked, sand hissing over it as the wind swept it like a housewife shooing dirt from her floor. No plants dared to peek their heads above ground. The only time you'd ever see a living plant in the open desert was at night.

The collective roar of the galloping steeds beat hard against Clye's ears, put a thrill in his chest.

The wind pulled at his curly hair, tried to lift his bowler hat. Clye put his right hand on his hat to keep it down, held the reigns in his left.

The adventure had begun.

THEY STOPPED FOR lunch after three hours of riding hard. Esta dug a few iron stakes out of her saddlebags and tied the steeds up to them. The animals clawed at the sand, digging up a few roots and sleeping plants. Meanwhile, the rest of the posse huddled around a lonely piece of sandstone and fished lunches out of their packs.

Clye wandered over to his cathrahd, scratched the steed behind its ears. His mind ambled back to when he was a young lad trapped at home.

"What you do puts a spot on your name," his mother would say. "Will it be a bright spot or a dark spot?" Clye had proceeded to ask her if running away would qualify as a dark spot and she promptly answered, "Yes, by hona!" and repented next Holy Day for swearing.

Outlawry: dark spot. Saving Jute from Justin Croy and the Proyton Gang: bright spot. He just hoped it'd be bright enough.

"Sandwalker don't let me fail," he murmured.

"Who ya talkin' to?"

Clye spun around to face Esta standing a few yards away with her hands on her hips.

"No one," Clye said, realizing that his hand had once again dropped to his empty holster.

The older woman glanced down at his hand, smiled. "Looks like they took your gun," she said.

Clye shrugged. "Nothin' I can do about it."

Esta nodded, adjusted her hat. She glanced out at the desert. Clye followed her gaze. On the horizon, the brown, craggy mountains poked up at the sky like bony fingers trying to claw the sun down. Nearer the mountains, the dune fields marched toward the posse, massive waves of sand like the seas of myths. Clye couldn't tell where the flat desert ended and the dunes began, since rippling waves of desert heat obscured his vision.

Esta grunted, then tipped her hat. Slowly, she turned to Clye. "You want a gun?"

Clye raised an eyebrow. "Yes, ma'am?"

Esta bent down and pulled a snub-nosed revolver from her boot. "Catch," she said, tossing the pistol to Clye as she rose up.

Clye caught it and looked the weapon over. The hilt was made of yellow bone with three leather thongs wrapped around it for grip. The barrel was chipped black metal, with obscure designs carved in it—signs that could spell either curses or blessings.

"This is a fine pistol," he murmured.

"Always need a weapon in the desert," Esta said. She turned back toward the dunes and mountains beyond. "You roam the desert much?"

Clye counted the rounds inside the revolver. Eight little lead bullets. Wonderful. He holstered the gun at his hip.

"Hey. You hear me?"

Clye glanced up. Esta had crossed her arms, frowning at him.

"Uh, yeah," Clye answered, "I've lived in the desert most of my life."

"Ah." Esta smiled. "Ranger, hunter, or outlaw?"

"Ranger," Clye said without thinking. He immediately blushed—wished his hat was the flat, wide-brimmed hat of a ranger instead of the sad, round bowl of a bartender's hat.

Esta cocked an eyebrow, then smirked. "Alright, Ranger," she said, drawing a revolver from her side, "let's see you shoot."

She stepped out a little ways onto the sand, bent down, and

picked up a small brown rock. She spit on it, and the rock turned nearly three shades darker. Straightening, she threw it out into the desert. A dusty cloud splashed up where it landed fifty paces away. Clye squinted. He could just see it lying with a little crater of sand encircling it.

Esta brought her gun to target with a smooth, almost galloping flourish. She fired and let the gun ride all the way back before firing again. When the dust cleared, a piece of the stone had been broken off. Esta nodded, twirled her gun, and holstered it.

A small chorus of applause went up behind them. The whole posse clapped.

Kobe shouted, "Noice shot there, ma'am!"

Esta looked at Clye. "Now your turn."

Clye frowned and stepped up beside her. Esta stepped back a few paces, folded her arms.

Clye loosened his shoulders, hunched down, stared at the stone—fifty paces away. He snatched the gun out of his holster, fired the moment the stone and sights aligned, tucked the pistol back against his chest until the dust cleared. The stone was split into about four pieces. Clye nodded and holstered his revolver.

There was no applause, but Clye didn't care. It was a keining good shot! He turned to Esta.

"Well?" he said, a smirk creeping onto his lips.

Esta smiled, eyes twinkling in the desert sun. "You're an outlaw," she said.

Clye's smirk vanished. "What?"

"An outlaw lives by his gun. He keeps it close to his heart, muscles it into the target, always fires immediately." Esta

68

pulled her revolver from her hip. "If you were a ranger, you would've done it like this."

She straightened her arm, pistol rigid in it like just another finger. "Pow," she whispered, faked a slight recoil and snapped the pistol straight again.

She holstered the revolver with a smile. "A ranger's gun is his servant. He points, he shoots, he holsters."

Esta walked up to Clye and grabbed his arm. Her eyebrows knit, dark eyes boring into his. "What's an outlaw doin' with a posse?" she whispered.

"I'm savin' my name," Clye snapped. He yanked his arm away. "Sheriff Quave agreed to clear it if I caught Justin Croy."

Esta frowned. "I see," she said. "But will that clear your name in there?" She pointed at his chest.

Clye shrugged his shoulders, looked down at the sand. *Yes. Yes it will*, he thought. His breathing strained. A coughing fit took him. Clye doubled over coughing, beating his chest.

"Kein! Kein!" he swore. "Stop it!"

His lungs loosened, he could breathe deeper. Clye looked around at the posse, who all stared at him. *Hona,* he thought.

Hollin, who was smoking a cigar and had his feet propped up on the sandstone rock, blew a smoke ring in Clye's direction. "On the grains, eh?" he chuckled. "Hear they're mighty bad for ya."

"Sure they are," Clye shot back. "I'm sure those cigars work wonders for the lungs."

Hollin's laughter stopped instantly. Smoke shot from his nose, pooled in his lap. "We've all made choices, Mr. Outlaw. And it's the wise that stick by 'em, no matter the consequences. Can't change nature."

Clye frowned. *Change nature.* Clye shook his head, turned his gaze toward the waiting mountains.

"Alright, posse," he said, "Let's get goin'. See if we can make the dune fields by nightfall."

# EIGHT

# APPLES

THEY MADE IT a few leagues into the dune fields when the sun set and the moon rose. Clye rolled himself up on the salra mat in the shadow of his cathrahd. He was glad to have a pistol at his side again. He fell asleep in the light of a frowning full moon, the ancient prayer on his lips. "…Guard my name with your whirlwinds. Guard my name…"

THE MOUNTAINS ROSE above the galloping posse, their sharp peaks stabbing at the clear blue sky. Some greenery was visible on the rocky slopes—seen but never enjoyed by up-standing folk. Only the bravest outlaws, and fiercest beasts, and living skeletons dwelt in the mountains.

Kobe led them forward, the posse now only a rifle's shot away from the stony toes of the mountains. A lump of reddish mountain stretched out from the range, a massive hole gaping at its base like a smiling, toothless grandmother. Looking up, Clye could see the lumpy mass of the mountain easing back into the hard spikes of the others.

Kobe reined in his cathrahd several yards before the mine

entrance. Clye trotted his steed up beside him.

"What are we lookin' at?" Clye asked, eyes on the boy.

Kobe pointed down at three guards standing beside an empty wooden desk, just inside the mine entrance. They were bearded, dressed in leather vests and mining caps, each gripping a pike in their gloved fingers. From Clye's height atop the cathrahd, the guards looked small and unimpressive.

One of the guards looked up at Kobe and smiled. "Oi, Kobe! Been good?"

"Alroight," Kobe returned, trotting his cathrahd a little nearer to the guards.

The guard stroked his beard with his free hand. "Who're them?"

"Sheriff sent a posse," Kobe said, hooking a thumb back at Clye and the others.

The guard frowned. "Whoy's that?"

"We're here to catch Justin Croy and the Proyton Gang," Clye spoke up. He tipped his hat to the guard. "I'm Clye Galler. I'd like to lead my posse into your mine. Is that alright with you?"

The guard curled his fingers tighter around his spear. "Oi'd prefer if you didn't. Proyton ain't in our moine, zurr, and that's a fact. We guard it too well."

Clye held up a finger. "I don't mean any disrespect, sir. But Sheriff Quave commissioned us to catch Justin Croy. And we think this is where he went."

The guard nodded to his fellow. "Foine. Look if ye must. We ain't got stables for 'at many steeds, though. You'll have to leave 'em outsoide."

"Very well." Clye dismounted, and the rest of the posse followed suit.

They tied up the steeds by the side of the mine entrance, and Kobe led the way into the mine.

Coiter Mine sprawled out into the dark, massive holes splitting the walls, floor, and ceiling as if giants had had a gunfight there. Ladders led up into the ceiling's holes, tracks went into the wall passages, and rope bridges spanned across the chasms in the floor. The mine was all gritty sandstone the color of blood—Clye had seen Justin Croy once split a boulder made of stone the same color using only sand power. Even the most skilled sand user was spent after using that much concentration.

The hole of the mine spread out wide like the throat of a dragon, stone mouth open both taller and wider than the Jute Law House.

Kobe padded away down the stone floor of the mine, pausing ahead as he came to a swaying rope bridge over a hole in the ground. Even from a distance Clye could see that the hole was wide enough to swallow a cathrahd or two easily. Kobe strode out onto the planks, barely touching the support ropes. He stopped on the other side, waiting.

When Clye came to the bridge, he did more than touch the support ropes, glancing down every few seconds in order to feel his stomach turn at the horrifying depth of it. The clang of pickaxes echoed from the darkness below.

"This way," Kobe said when everyone had crossed. He scampered off to the right-hand wall of the mine, footsteps echoing.

The stone began to slope, and rubble dotted the path. This seemed to be a well-used track the miners followed beside this wall—Clye noticed cart tracks etched into the sandstone.

Kobe kept his hand on the wall, though the floor was as wide as the massive mouth of the mine. Clye trotted over to him, placing his hand on the wall as well. Esta and the others came up behind.

Kobe marched forward, back straight, shoulders back. Clye smiled.

"You like workin' in the mine?" Clye said.

"Sometoimes," Kobe answered, without looking back.

"How's your mother?"

"She's well." Kobe's voice dropped, though his pace quickened. "She is very old, zurr Cloye. Old and alone."

Clye fell silent.

They walked on, the cavern growing darker as they went. The white crystal on Kobe's cap grew brighter as the mine became darker. Kobe said the light inside the crystal came from a special mushroom they harvested for the helmets.

"We moight foind some growin'," he said. "You can smear 'em on your forehead, but don't eat 'em. Poisonous."

The slope of the mine floor grew ever steeper, and massive holes at times left only a three-foot ledge for the posse to walk on. Soon the light of Kobe's cap was all that could be seen.

"Ey! How much further?" The voice of one of Hollin's hunters.

"Some ways, zurr," Kobe called back. "It's near the 'bandoned Upper Lower shaft when oi heard the voices last."

"Upper Lower shaft," one of the other hunters muttered.

They reached the floor of the mine after what felt like an eternity of walking. Torches on the walls filled the place enough to see, and the clang of miners working overwhelmed the air. The space was huge and open as a town square, and tunnels led away into the walls. The floor was black as if it had been burnt. Clye was surprised at the heat that soaked up through his boots as he walked on it.

He asked Kobe about the phenomenon.

The boy smiled. "Noice, eh? It's foiery dragons as live in the core, it is."

"That's a miner's tale," Clye said.

Kobe shrugged. "Maybe. But who would know the core better 'an moiners?"

Kobe led the posse into one of the small tunnels, greeting the miners they passed. Clye could almost brush the ceiling of the reddish tunnel shaft if he stretched his arm out. Kobe picked up a spare pickax from the floor and stuck it in his belt. The white glow of the miners' caps illuminated the tunnel. A little way in, a ladder led up into the sandy ceiling. Kobe stopped, pointed to the ladder, smiled.

"Upper Lower," he said.

Kobe started up the wooden ladder, each rung creaking as the boy put his weight on it. Clye swallowed, then started up it himself. Up the ladder he went—up into darkness. Clye felt the temperature drop as he climbed, felt the wall every few feet to make sure it was still there. Only a sliver of light dropped down to him from Kobe's lamp.

Then the light vanished. Clye kept his breathing even, tried to see in the blackness around him. His eyes had adjusted somewhat, but not enough to see more than a vague circle of the round sandstone shaft.

"Sandwalker help me," he murmured, climbing farther up the ladder.

Clye reached out for another rung, but found only the stone wall. Light suddenly filled the space, blinding him. He twisted around, swiped at nothing, almost lost his balance.

"That you, Kobe?" Clye snapped, eyes shut to keep out the painful light.

"Oy, zurr," the boy replied. "Oi'm roight here, zurr Cloye. Jump toward the sound of moy voice—you'll land safe on the Upper Lower floor."

Clye's muscles tensed. He shook his head in the darkness. "Kein you, hona adventurous kive!"

A chuckle. "Them's lot o' swears in one spout."

Clye smiled, pushed off from the ladder, tried to twist in midair. His hip struck stone, his arms and torso air. He started to fall, tried to grab at something, found Kobe's hand. The boy dragged him to his feet, and Clye dusted the sand from his breeches. Finally, his eyes adjusted to the light of Kobe's lamp. They stood in a rough horizontal tube, slightly slanted, the ceiling only inches above Clye's head. The lower end of the tunnel quickly ended in blood-red rock. But the upper end seemed to stretch on forever.

"Up there," Kobe whispered. "Once the others get up."

Esta and Jenaven had no trouble jumping from ladder to shaft floor—not so for Hollin and his hunters. One of them sprained their wrist on the stone. *That* was a holler if Clye'd ever heard one. They used the man's belt to tie the wrist up.

Kobe led the way up the tunnel. "Keep quoit," he put a finger to his lips. "List'n for the voices."

The light from his cap illuminated a good portion of the tunnel, and Clye stuck close to the mining boy. Clye felt the cold stone wall every few feet, leaning in to press his ear against the sandstone. All he could hear were distant taps coming from the miners below, and the occasional *drip* of water.

Ahead, Kobe got down on all fours, pressed his head to the shaft floor. His body tensed.

Clye walked up beside him, knelt down, and whispered, "What is it?"

Kobe lifted his face from the floor, turned to Clye. His dark eyes were narrowed in his round face. "The voices," he said.

Clye put his ear to the floor. Muffled echoes and vibrations drifted up through the rock in little bursts. They came in varied tones and rhythms. Voices for certain, though he could pick out no words.

Clye lifted his head up, scratched his chin. He turned to Kobe, squinting because of the light. "How far down?"

Kobe pursed his lips. "Least three feet o' rock. Take me more 'an a hour to get through. They'd hear afore I got two strokes in."

"Kein," Clye spat, looking at the floor. So close. "How does the gang get in there?"

Kobe shrugged. "Probably got a tunnel that leads down from the mountains."

Clye frowned. "Seems elaborate. They'd be safer if they stayed up on the mountainside in some cave. Only outlaws venture that close to the peaks—no one would find 'em."

"Oi don't know," Kobe said. "Maybe they're scared the skeletons will march down the slopes."

"Nah. They've never done that," Clye said.

"Well what are you two doing? Hatching a plan, eh? Or counting grains on the floor?" Hollin pushed in beside Clye, light glimmering off his golden tooth.

Kobe's eyebrows narrowed.

Clye cleared his throat. "We think Proyton Gang is below

us. We don't know how they got down there, and we can't dig down to 'em without causin' a racket and scarin' 'em away."

"Interesting, I like it," Hollin scratched at his sideburns. "They might have a hidden passage in the walls, you know."

Kobe shook his head. "They'd have to walk through the moine, and it's always guarded. The moiners would notice."

"Could the guards be bribed?" Hollin squinted.

"Never," Kobe snapped.

Clye ran his finger along the floor. Sandstone, like the rest of the mine. Very rough, grainy sandstone. Clye pursed his lips. Justin was terribly addicted to grains, but he knew the Way of Sand better than anyone. At fifteen Clye had watched him pull a boulder apart with sand power.

"Kobe," Clye said, eyes still on the floor, "do any of the miners ever dig with grains?"

Kobe wrinkled his nose. "Grains are filthy. Oi never seen a decent moiner use 'em."

Hollin patted Clye on the back. "I've seen a lot of strange things, Mr. Outlaw. But I've never seen anyone move sandstone with anything other than a pickax. Well, it has 'sand' in the name, but sandstone isn't *sand*, eh?"

"It was once." Clye scraped some of the loose grains off of the sandstone with his nails. "Stand back," he said as he got to his feet.

Kobe and Hollin backed off to stand with the rest of the posse.

Clye cupped the grains in his hand, put his hand to his face and inhaled the sand. Almost instantly his senses heightened. He could feel every nerve in the tips of his fingers, see every wrinkle of the stone in perfect detail. The floor looked so close and yet leagues away. He reached down toward it, tensed his muscles, felt that strange connection between himself and the sand. He felt that even this sandstone would obey him. It was like each grain that made up the stone below was now just another finger to him. Clye shut his eyes, lifted his hands. He could feel each grain of the sandstone lifting, separating—still connected by that same, strange force.

He broke out sweating. His muscles shook. *More, more*, he thought. Clye lifted his hands higher. He couldn't hear anything except for the drum, drum of blood in his ears.

His limbs shook uncontrollably. Clye grit his teeth, flung himself to the side, felt the connection break. His shoulder struck the floor. Clye could hear voices—louder voices. Some were scared, some angry. Were they the fears inside him, or were they the posse speaking? Or Proyton?

Clye inhaled, then coughed raggedly. He opened his eyes. A block of sandstone sat on the floor beside him, and a large hole had opened in the floor. Jenaven was jumping down into it, firing his long rifle. The mission. Redemption. Clye struggled to his feet, dizzy, blinking, stumbling. He shook his head and drew his pistol. He was the only one in the tunnel. Shouts and gunshots and a warm yellow glow diffused out of the hole in the floor. Clye looked down and saw Jenaven and Esta crouched behind an overturned table in the room below.

Clye grit his teeth, jumped down. He rolled to ease his fall, scampered into the shelter of the table between Jenaven and Esta. Jen gave Clye a nod and jumped up quickly to fire over the table.

Clye gripped a table-leg, shook his head, trying to clear the dizziness from his mind. He yanked himself up to peek over the table. The room was wide as a saloon and roughly round, full of kegs, tables, and barrels. A large crack split the sandstone in the far corner. Torches ringed the entire wall, and lamps swung from the stone ceiling. Brighter than daylight if not for the smoke and sand obscuring the air.

Clye saw the tip of a hat peeking out from behind a barrel. He aimed and fired. A curse and the hat ducked out of view. Clye ducked behind the table beside Jen. As he'd anticipated, a bullet went whining over the place where his head had just been.

"Dayer! You lead the retreat! I'll hold them off," someone shouted. Clye recognized the voice—Justin Croy.

A gruff reply: "They used yer 'scape route as an entrance. You wanna survive, you follow me an' get yerself outta here."

Clye peeked up over the rim of the table. Justin Croy stepped out from behind a stack of barrels, one hand holstering a revolver, the other holding the tip of his short-brimmed blacksmith's fedora.

Clye brought his pistol up and fired, barely aiming. The bullet went clear of Justin into the far wall. Justin froze where he stood, inhaling the sandy air. Suddenly all that sand was whirling, whirling so fast and so quick Clye couldn't keep his eyes open for the sting. He shut his eyes, fired once blindly.

Clye shut his mouth. The sand in the air was so thick. Clye was strong with grains, but nowhere near as strong as Justin. If he tried to fight, he'd lose all his strength again and fail to overcome Justin's storm. He was still weak from moving the sandstone.

What could he do? The storm swirled faster, thicker every second. The table was little protection. Clye could feel the moisture being sucked out of his skin as each grain pummeled it. His lungs burned, cried for air. Clye could hear shouts and the roar of rushing feet. He inhaled slightly, felt the sand enter his lungs. He coughed—ragged, hacking coughs, the lungs throwing out all the air they had wanted to take in. He heard Esta coughing beside him.

Clye's senses heightened from the sand, but still he couldn't breathe. He could barely move. With all the strength he had left, Clye raised his gun. He reached out to the sand, trying to find where Justin—the storm's eye—was standing. He could feel it—feel the point around which the sand was turning. Clye aimed his gun at the spot that his mind was telling him, fired once, twice, kept firing until he heard the high, girlish scream of Justin Croy in pain.

The sand slowed, stopped striking his skin. Clye inhaled at last, desperate gulps of smoky, dusty air. But it was breathable. Another gunshot, but not Clye's. Another scream from Justin.

Clye opened his eyes, saw Justin kneeling on the ground, gripping his left forearm, which was covered in blood. There was a bloody tear in the side of his jacket, and his hat had been knocked off.

"*Kive*," Justin hissed, gaze locked on something in the corner of the room.

Clye jumped to his feet, knocking against Esta.

"Sorry," he said without looking. Pistol still in hand, Clye rushed around the table toward Justin. Jenaven didn't follow.

Clye approached Justin slowly, gun trained on the man's head. Justin breathed hard. He glanced up at Clye with angry red-rimmed eyes.

"Glad to see you again," Justin said, smiling. He suddenly winced, gripped his forearm harder. Clye noticed the little finger of his right hand had been cut off at the knuckle. Slowly, Justin's face relaxed. He nodded to Clye. "Don't delay it.

Shoot me, Lyle." He exhaled, nodded again. "Sorry about Ross—I know he loved you. He's dead now, though."

Clye grit his teeth, hand trembling. *Good riddance*, he thought. Ross almost killed him when he was nearest to redeeming his name. And Justin had sent him. Clye tightened his grip on the trigger, stopped, shook his head. Justin was to be imprisoned, not killed. That was the deal. That was how he redeemed his name—successfully this time.

Clye kept his gun trained on Justin, but gazed at the floor. Clye scooped the blacksmith's fedora off the ground, set it on the outlaw's head. Justin looked up, eyebrow cocked.

"No man should be without a hat, 'specially when ladies are present," Clye said. He smirked, nodded back to where Esta and Jenaven had been crouched behind the table.

Justin smiled. "I always liked you, Lyle." He winced.

Clye glanced down at the wound. Clye had shot him in the soft part of the forearm near the elbow crease. The skin had been torn and a large vein was pumping blood as hard as it could out of the tear.

"Let me borrow your knife," Clye said, holding a hand out to Justin. "I'll cut up my shirt to bind your wound."

Justin glanced down at Clye's hand, frowned. "Neither Proyton or Yeller codes would allow for that," he said.

Kein. Always by the book. Clye took a step away from Justin, turned slightly so he could scan the rest of the room. The outlaws were nowhere to be seen. Hollin and his hunters had risen, standing behind kegs of beer. Kobe crouched in a corner, revolver raised. Esta stood behind the table, frowning.

"Esta!" Clye called. "Bring a rope over here. I got 'im."

Esta glanced down at the table, shook her head.

Clye frowned. "What's wrong? We got our man, let's go."

Esta kicked the table in front of her. It tipped down, revealing the slumped corpse of Jenaven, rifle still gripped in his dry hands.

Clye spun around to Justin, heat unbidden rising in his chest. "You killed him," Clye spat, all thought and eloquence vanishing. "Why'd you kill him?"

Justin frowned. "What are you talking about, Lyle? This was a gunfight. People die."

Clye grit his teeth, the pistol in his hand wavering. He hated Jen—didn't he?

Justin continued. "He was a hunter by the hat. Murderer. Protected by law. It's unjust. He finally got what his crimes always demanded."

Clye lowered his gun, surprised by the lump in his throat. He glanced over to the stack of barrels that Justin had been standing behind. The barrels had fallen over, and apples had spilled out onto the sandstone. Clye walked over, stooped down and picked one up. Red as blood. Shimmering in the torchlight. He took a bite, the sweet juice dripping into his mouth, moistening his parched lips. Liquid victory, hidden behind blood-red skin. Perhaps that was the magic of an apple. That if you went through the blood—through the death, through the gunfight—you would find sweetness. Victory. Clye took another bite.

Justin looked up at him and smiled. "How many apples have you stolen?" he said.

## NINE

# EMPTY NOOSE

CLYE LED JUSTIN into the town square, the posse following behind him.

The town square sat empty as a beggar's bowl except for two young boys playing around the gallows. Clye paused in his procession, hand still firm on Justin Croy's shoulder.

The two boys were taking turns throwing a ball through the now-empty loop of the noose. Mostly the throws struck the rope, making it swing chaotically. The noose seemed so light when the ball struck it—so heavy when a body was strung from it.

"Well, Mr. Outlaw, are you going to go in or not?"

Clye twisted to see Hollin standing beside him, smile on his lips.

"Course I am," Clye returned. "Move," he grunted to Justin.

The posse walked forward in a slow, halting march toward the steps of the Law House. Hollin's three hunters had left— already paid out of Hollin's own pocket. Clye walked Justin up the stairs to the narrow Law House door.

"Open it," Clye said.

Justin chuckled. "You're about to imprison me. I'm not going to make it easier for you. Get the door yourself."

"I could shoot you dead right now."

Justin shook his head—slowly, haltingly. "Lyle," he said, "you know we both deserve worse than that."

Clye bit his lip, tension building in his chest. *Don't let them hang him,* Clye prayed, *no matter how much the murderer deserves it.* Murder. Jen. Dead on the sandstone with a hole in his head. Clye's nostrils flared, trying to suck more air into lungs that suddenly felt constricted. He didn't want to do this—but there was only room for one neck in Quave's noose, and it wouldn't be Clye's. He grit his teeth. "Open the door, Justin!"

Justin moved his bound hands up to the brass door handle and turned it awkwardly. The door opened a little, and Justin shoved it open the rest of the way with his boot. Clye pushed on Justin's back and the two stumbled into the building.

Sheriff Quave sat at his desk shoved against the right-hand wall, scribbling something on his pile of papers. Clye cleared his throat, and the sheriff looked up.

"Back so soon?" The frown beneath his pure-white mustache suddenly turned into a grin. He shoved his chair back and jumped to his feet, strode forward.

"I knowed you'd get 'im!" Quave said, pushing Justin aside and shaking Clye's hand heartily.

"It was an honor, Sheriff," Clye answered, yanked his hand away. The cut on his thumb throbbed.

"Uh course, uh course." Quave craned his neck to see around Clye to the rest of the posse. "Nice posse ya got there," Quave frowned. "Where's my hunter?"

Hollin pushed forward, nudged Clye aside. He removed his hat with a flourish and clutched it to his chest. "He died, Your Majesty," he bowed, then quickly reddened. "Uh, uh, Mr. Sheriff, I mean, if you understand. It's not often, of course, that I'm in the presence of such a—"

"Shut up, Wesner." Quave's eyebrows were slanted so sharply they hid his eyes entirely. His lips quivered. "I don't wanna see your face in this establishment again unless it's tongue-less, ya hear?"

Hollin planted his hat back on his head. "Sir, of course." He gave a salute, turned and marched back with the rest of the posse.

Clye shoved Justin Croy toward Quave. "Sheriff, here's your man. Lock 'im up. Then you'll clear my name, give these folks their reward, and I'll walk out of this office free as a bird. Got it?"

"I understand." Quave was quiet as he grabbed Justin's bound hands, walked him over to the cell in the far wall. He yanked the cell door open and shoved the outlaw in.

Quave snapped the door shut and locked it with a large key. "That's your home fer the next two weeks. Then we hang ya. You like that, hunter-murderin' outlaw?"

Justin said nothing.

The sheriff walked over to his desk and sat down on the chair. He grabbed his quill pen and started scribbling on a sheet of paper, shoulders slumped.

Clye narrowed his eyes, folded his arms. He turned to Esta and Kobe and Hollin standing on the steps holding the door open, motioned for them to come in. They stepped inside just enough for the door to close behind them. Esta looked from Clye to the sheriff, shook her head. Kobe kept his head down.

"Sheriff Quave!" Clye said.

Quave looked up from his desk. His eyes were red-rimmed and watery, but his teeth were grit. "Yes?"

"Your agreement, sir."

"What agreement? We wrote nothing."

Clye sucked in a breath. *No.* His eyes drifted to the long revolver holstered at Quave's hip. A throbbing beat through Clye's thumb. Clye curled his fists, angled his eyebrows. "We sealed it in blood!" he shouted, pointing to the scar on his thumb. "If you're a man of honor you *will* clear my name!"

Sheriff Quave clasped his hands together, elbows on the desktop. He nodded slowly, eyebrows knit. "I understand, Mr. Outlaw. But you're a dangerous man. I can't just let ya go like that real easy."

"You swore!"

"You killed my bounty hunter," snapped the sheriff, blue eyes blazing. He unclasped his hands, curled them into fists.

Clye grit his teeth, took a step toward Quave. "Justin Croy killed your hunter. And he'll hang for that. But I'm innocent. I upheld my side of the deal, you keep yours."

Quave glared at Clye. His fingers brushed his revolver hilt, then withdrew. He shook his head, turned to his beloved papers. He snatched one from the far side of his desk, scanned it, scratched something on it, then threw it to Clye.

Clye grabbed the paper out of the air, began to scan it himself.

"It's your record," Quave said, "Clear. Signed. Now get outta here."

Clye folded the paper and stuffed it in his pocket. "Not until you give these folks the reward money."

The sheriff shook his head, jotted something on another paper. "Here," he handed it to Clye. "Jist take this to the bank with a 'wanted' poster for Justin Croy. You'll get your money. Filthy kives," he added.

Clye straightened, turned, handed the paper to Esta, and marched out the door, down the steps into the square.

"You're not going with us?"

Clye spun around to see Esta, Kobe, and Hollin crowded in the doorway looking out at him.

"Where are you going?" Esta said.

Clye paused, looked out beyond the gallows at the buildings ringing the square. Posters were tacked onto most of them—no advertisements, just wanted posters. Faces. Faces of men and women who'd hang if Law or upstanding citizen found them.

Clye bit his lip, surprised by the bit of moisture that sprang up behind his eyes. He turned to the posse standing on the doorstep of the Law House. "I'm gonna tear down all my wanted posters. I'm a free man, now. Lyle Yeller doesn't exist in the name of the law."

"Hey kid?" Hollin raised a hand. "You want your job back, you know, now that you're clear? We can forge our new reputations together, eh?"

*Job. Reputations.* Clye smiled, nodded. "Alright."

Clye turned and walked out of the town square, past the gallows and the two boys playing under them.

# TEN
# PAUL GALLER

"HERE YOU ARE, SIR." Clye set an iron platter piled with potatoes and onions down on the table in front of the regular. It had been three days since Justin was imprisoned. He was scheduled to hang in a week-and-a-half.

The shaggy-bearded regular looked up from beneath a black fedora and smiled a toothless grin. "Fank 'ee," he said, spittle dribbling onto his beard.

Clye smiled, bowed. "Of course."

Turning around, he saw a newcomer leaning against the bar, croaking, "Bartender!"

Clye straightened. He strode up behind the counter and looked the man in the eyes. "How can I help you?"

The newcomer scratched his massive sideburns, rolled his eyes. "I want a pint of white valagu, Darky."

Clye grabbed a bottle off the shelf behind him. "The name's Clye," he bent down and fished a pint glass out from underneath the counter. "You can call me 'Clye' or 'Bartender' or 'Sir.' That clear?"

The newcomer glanced down at Clye's hand as he poured the

liquor into the glass. He flashed a yellow smile. "Real clear."

Clye nodded stiffly. "That'll be fourteen kaj."

As the man tugged out his purse, the saloon doors burst open and a mailman in a gray cap walked through, a large satchel on his hip. He held up an envelope, sunlight from the windows reflecting off of the wax seal.

"Letter for Clye Galler!" he called.

Clye paused as he returned the bottle to the shelf on the wall. Quave hadn't let him read his parents' first envelope, so Clye had written them again with the wonderful news—their son alive, free, respectable.

The newcomer had already walked away. Clye picked the copper kaj out of the angoraeth fur and placed them in the money jar beneath the counter.

"Letter for Clye Galler?" the mailman sounded sad as he scanned the room, waving the envelope.

Clye raised his hand. He came out from behind the bar. "That's me."

The mailman nodded, handed him the letter, then turned and walked out of the saloon.

Clye adjusted his hat, snapped open the red seal on the letter, and read it right there in the middle of the saloon.

> *Oh honey,*
>
> *I'm glad you're alright. I can't visit. I am very busy with the mourning ceremonies.*
> *Your pa loved you.*
>
> *Lovin,*
> *Ma*

Clye froze. The clanging and singing and talking—all the sounds of the saloon suddenly muted.

Clye crumpled up the letter in his hands, threw it at the wall. It bounced off—fell dejected in a corner.

He screamed, ripped his hat off. There were no words. It shouldn't have happened this way. He should have been by Pa, prayed for him in his last moments. But now—his support was gone. His love was gone. His pa was gone.

Clye glanced around the room, breathing hard. Most of the men had risen, most of the women and children cowered at their tables. Clye shook his head. What the kein was he doing?

Clye scooped up his hat from off the ground, placed it on his head. "Sorry, folks," he said, nodded to one of the families. "I need a walk."

He pushed open the saloon doors and walked out onto the sand.

CLYE DIDN'T KNOW how long he walked. His head was tangled with anger and shock like endlessly coiling snakes. In his proudest moment, his parents weren't there. In their lowest moment, *Clye* wasn't there. He tugged the pouch of western grains out of his pocket and snuffed a few to ease the pain, but it only made it worse. Angry as hona with all the senses hyper-active? That didn't seem like peace.

Clye kicked the tumbleweeds as they crossed his path. When a beggar tugged at his leg asking for alms, Clye cast sand at him.

*Had* he redeemed his name? There was no Law after him, but he was no hero. At church, no one shook his hand. When the minister announced the news that Justin Croy was imprisoned, no one cheered. All they did was talk about the sentence.

Clye's parents always loved him, but now his pa was gone. Ma would be too concerned with mourning to show her son love. How can you show someone else love when all you have is sadness?

Clye blinked up at the blue summer sky. He was crying. Fat, yellowy tears mixed with the dust on his face and ran off the edge of his chin.

"Pa," he whispered, shutting his eyes. The bald head, the round face, the toy pistol he'd brought home when Clye was just six.

"Cowboy, Pa? Can we play 'cowboy?'" Pa would smile, ruffle Clye's hair, then get down on all fours and neigh like an imbval. They'd hustle around the yard together, Pa bucking and pretending to be a wild imbval while Clye chased him with the toy pistol, swinging a piece of thread. They'd play for hours like that when Clye was little.

Clye shook his head. *Over. All over.* Those dreaded words. "We can't play anymore. We're done now. Run off and finish your chores."

"Howdy, partner."

Clye's eyes shot open. His hand shot to his hip and he looked around. He had come to the end of the market street, was standing a few yards away from the fence and stalls that contained Esta's steeds. Esta herself leaned against the fence, chewing on a piece of straw.

Clye straightened, hoped she couldn't see his tears. "Howdy."

Esta took the straw out of her mouth, pointed it toward Clye's face. "What's wrong?" Her tone had softened.

"Nothing." Clye was startled by how shaky his voice came out.

"Liar. What happened?"

Clye shook his head. He looked at the cathrahds pawing in the pen. "I gotta go home. Just for a while, just until…"

Esta frowned. "Son, what happened?"

Clye's gaze fell to the sand. "I…my…my Pa…" he ground his teeth to keep the sobs back.

"Look up, son."

Teeth clenched, Clye looked up at Esta's dark, wrinkled face. Her deep, almost black eyes bored into Clye. They seemed to probe the depths of his soul. But there was kindness in them—a bird's heart looking through those eyes. Clye didn't feel like she was searching him to dissect or operate or pick out some filth to examine. It seemed like she was searching in hopes of finding some gold buried beneath the outlaw sands.

"Mister," she said at last, "you don't know who you are. You won't find your healing in a job or people. You find it in the footprints of the Sandwalker. I'll tell ya what…" She motioned to the pen behind her. "I'll letcha borrow one of these steeds—go visit home. When ya come back, I'll give ya a job on the ranch—teach ya what I know. How's that?"

Clye looked out at the desert and the rising mountains beyond. Wind blew the sand into quivering clouds in the distance, obscuring the sky in some places like bloodstains on an outlaw shirt.

Clye exhaled. "Thank you. But I ain't sure if I'll come back."

Esta smiled, tipped her hat. "You will, Mister."


IT WAS A three-day ride to Annaday. Clye arrived the middle of the afternoon the third day.

He reigned the loaned cathrahd to a halt in front of his parents' white cottage. His chest tightened.

In the middle of Ma's lush green yard sat a black, dome-shaped rock, the sunlight glinting off its polished surface. Clye leaped off the cathrahd, jumped the fence, and knelt down in front of the stone.

Letters had been hewn into the stone—a sharp, pointed serif, so deep they looked like Hona's Gates even in the afternoon sun. Clye ran his fingers over them.

"Kein," he said, quiet, without emphasis or anger. Tears welled up in his eyes, and his throat felt constricted.

*Paul Galler. 3114-3189. Husband. Father.*

Clye placed both his hands on the stone, gripped it till his arms shook. Tears rolled down his cheeks. The grass poked at the knees of his breeches, the shadow of his hat darkening his face. The air felt warmer than it had moments ago, and the tears were so hot they brought no cool to Clye's sweltering skin.

Shaking, Clye released the headstone and gripped the brim of his hat. It burned his hands—or was it his hands that were already boiling? Clye ripped the bartender's hat from his head and tore the sacred fabric apart. There was nothing sacred but the bones of his dead pa. Breathing hard, he looked at the shreds in his hands. No hat. No pa. No name.

He cast the shreds to the ground, let out the scream that was bottled in his chest.

Clye shut his eyes. "Pa," he croaked, pressing his forehead to the scorching black rock. The pain was almost comfort—to be able to feel something real, feel something that cut through the hot, black fog that hugged his soul.

"What the hona are you doin', boy?"

Clye whipped his head up, wiped his tears on his sleeve.

His mother stood on the porch, draped in a black dress and veil. The veil was so dark Clye could've almost imagined the fanged face of death itself hiding within, instead of the strong, wrinkled face of his mother. She crossed her arms.

"You leave that rock alone, ya hear?" she said.

"Ma," Clye rose to his feet, tears welling afresh in his eyes.

Ma held up her hand. "I'm in mournin'. I cain't help ya. If *you* boy have some comfort for an old lady, bring it up. Otherwise you jist turn yo'self around and head on home."

"This is home." Clye said.

His mother stood still as a statue, the wind rustling her veil and the shadowed hem of her dress.

Clye glanced down at the silent gravestone, then up at his silent mother. "Why didn't you tell me he was sick?"

"Pa didn't want you to worry." It came out flat, forced.

Clye sighed, nodded. He knew his ma. It was she who hadn't wanted him to worry, because if he worried about Pa, Clye would stay with them, and bring the Law to her door with his outlaw stench. When Ma said she was concerned for Clye, she was concerned for her own safety.

And yet, wasn't that fair? Wasn't he an outlaw with a mountain of crimes worthy of both hanging and drawing? She was right to fear for her safety—to deny love in favor of life. And even then, she had shown some love, when she could.

But it was all over now. Pa was dead. Ma was loveless.

Clye looked up at his mother standing on the porch, immovable as the image of a dead king hewed in stone. He opened his mouth, then shut it. Clye's eyes fell to the black rock at his feet—a single spot on Ma's perfect lawn.

*Paul Galler. 3114-3189. Husband. Father.*

Clye couldn't keep the tears back. But he held the sobs. He looked up at Ma, teeth clenched. He nodded. Like Ma requested, Clye turned himself around and headed on home.

But Clye Galler had no home. No home, no job, no parents.

Grown man and former outlaw though he was, Clye never cried as much as he did those three days galloping back to Jute on the back of that cathrahd.

# ELEVEN

# SNAKES CAN WIELD LASSOS

CLYE WALKED UP the steps and into the saloon, his un-covered black hair almost shiny in the afternoon sun.

He'd returned the cathrahd to Esta earlier that morning after he'd returned from Annaday. "You wanna become a cowboy?" she'd asked, to which Clye had hastily replied, "I don't wanna be nothin'. I work at the saloon, and I might as well work there till I die." Esta had smiled. "I have a feelin' you'll be back."

Clye pushed through the batwing doors, kept his head down and wove between the tables and chairs. He shoved open the kitchen door.

All the cooks looked at him with wide eyes. "What're you doin' here, son?" one of them asked.

"I'm still bartender here, ain't I?"

The cook shook her head. "Mr. Wesner replaced you the day you left."

Clye clenched his fists. *Kein that man!* He glanced at the staircase in the corner, rushed up it.

At the top of the staircase stood a single wooden door with a pearl handle like a single dragon's eye. Clye paused, remembered Hollin's gold-toothed smile. He was a generous man, he'd help. With a nod, he turned the handle.

It was a massive wood-paneled room, completely empty except for a desk near the far wall. Hollin sat at the desk, talking with a man holding up a large parchment.

The moment Clye stepped into the room, Hollin jumped to his feet with a shout.

"Hey! I told you only on a Sixth Day, was that not correct?"

Clye stopped where he stood, straightened. "I thought you said I could keep my job here. We'd forge our reputations together."

Hollin walked out from behind his desk, shoved the parchment man aside. "Only a *Sixth Day,* Outlaw," he hissed.

"Are you gonna answer me?"

Hollin stopped three feet short of Clye. He drew a short pistol from his pocket. "Let me put it this way. Emotions and business don't mix. If you would've walked it off for say, an hour, things might've turned out differently. But to leave town—" Hollin shook his head, clucked his tongue. "Very bad. Now I'm gonna have to ask you to leave my office."

"My pa died!" Clye bit his lip, eyes burning. He hadn't meant for it to come out.

Hollin paused where he stood, tapped his pale chin. "You know I'm sorry to hear that. Terrible thing to lose a father, I lost one myself, eh?" Hollin toyed with his short pistol. "Was your father killed by a gun-wound?"

Clye's fingers itched for his own pistol, but Hollin was already raising his silver snub-nose.

Clye turned and fled. A gunshot split the air next to his ear. Clye ran out of the room and down the stairs. Another gunshot—Clye heard it ping off the door handle. When he reached the foot of the stairs, Clye glanced at the wide-eyed faces of the cooks and rushed out of the saloon.

"BACK SO SOON?" Esta walked up to the fence and put her hands on her hips. Her eyes sparkled.

Clye scratched the back of his head, turned and looked at the street. The breeze blew a bit of sand in the air. It rained down on an empty food stall. The grains sprinkled off the roof of the stall, raining down on the street till they vanished. Plucked up. Dropped. Buried.

*Buried.* That was something—hide away from the gaze of those who saw his filth. Dig himself beneath the sands and dry out into bones.

But no. Esta said she'd give him a job on her ranch. That was something else. Maybe it could wring a stain or two off his name. It was worth the try.

Clye looked up at Esta with her sweeping cowboy hat. He inhaled. "I'll take the job," he said. "No pay—I just need to keep busy."

"Course," Esta returned, nodding. "I never said a thing 'bout pay. This is me teachin' you to get your keinin' head out of the ground. I'll train you to be a cowboy, and I'll show you the Living Sands."

"What the hona is that?"

Esta smiled, tipped her hat. "You'll have to find out, Mister. Say, your name was Clye, right?"

"Yes'm."

Esta nodded. "Good name. Means winter sunrise—all misty an' obscured. You can't really tell if it's risin', but risin' it is."

Clye shook his head. "I'm a sunset, ma'am—no risin'."

"You *wanna* rise?"

"Course. Who the hona wouldn't."

Clye looked down at his boots, noticing the serpents embossed on the leather. He'd met quite a number of snakes in his day. The Yellers themselves were named after the Cahzi Yelling Snake. Terrifying animal—broad flat head, massive fangs, and a piercing scream that shook the desert rocks. Most of the time it would stay silent, try to slither over the dust like a friendly sand snake. But any time it was scared—scream, ruckus, poisonous bite. No matter where it went, it couldn't escape its foul nature. Even when silent, animals avoided it—remembering the scream.

Clye shook his head. No job could save him. Even if it took some tarnish off of his name, it could never change his outlaw nature. Perhaps it was not just Lyle Yeller that was damned to rot in Hona. Perhaps it was Clye Galler, too.

Clye felt a firm hand on his shoulder. He pulled away, reeled back, and whipped out his snub-nosed revolver. Esta stood, frowning, her own pistol out.

"Put that gun down, son," she said. "You never had someone comfort ya before? It's human."

Clye holstered the pistol. "I changed my mind. I'm not taking the job."

Esta raised an eyebrow. "I thought you wanted to keep busy?"

"Doesn't matter," Clye shrugged. "My name is still blacker 'an igru's dung. There's no savin' it."

"You ain't no outlaw," Esta said. "You cleared your name. I was there, remember? So cut this nonsense. The only thing black about you is your skin."

Clye looked down, a smile creeping onto his lips. "Maybe I will take your job."

"Good." Esta holstered her pistol, crossed her arms. "I'll have Betty run the shop, and I'll take you back to the ranch. Got some wenkiids that need breaking—easy work. It's catching 'em that's the hard part."

"Wenkiids?" Clye exclaimed.

Esta grinned. "We get 'em *wild*, son. Not to brag, but there ain't many cowboys as good as Esta Galthor."

Clye smiled. He glanced out at the desert where the wind was whipping the sand off the dunes. Sweeping. Falling. Getting up again.

A hand on his shoulder. Clye turned slowly. Esta's dark eyes looked into his.

"Clye," she said, "I don't give a kein about your name, and neither does the Sandwalker."

She patted his shoulder and walked away.

Clye stood there a moment. He let the smile remain on his face. With a sigh, he turned and followed the cowboy.

CLYE AND ESTA rode out to the ranch on one of her imbvals. Esta rode with her knees tucked against the antelope's strong neck, steering the beast by grabbing its twisted horns. Clye sat right behind her, gripping the fleecy beast's gray side with his knees while holding onto the old lady's waist.

It was about a half hour ride out to Esta's ranch, the time passing in complete silence. The ranch was a large house nestled in an outcropping of boulders, painted with pale desert browns. It had a wide, sweeping roof with wooden shingles. In the front jutted a covered porch with two rocking chairs on it. To the right of the house Clye could see a massive animal pen with a few green-scaled wenkiids in it. Hugging the boulder crop behind the pen were rows of barns, each shingled, each painted.

Esta trotted the imbval up to the porch and abruptly slid off, dragging Clye with her. He fell to the sand, chuckled, looked up to see Esta jogging up the steps to the porch. It had been a long time since he'd been alone with a lady. Clye jumped to his feet and rushed after her.

Esta made it about halfway up the porch when the front door swung open.

Clye stopped; Esta kept walking. In the doorway stood an old, pale-skinned man with a massive gray beard. He wore a brown homesteader's derby and a faded blue jacket. He gripped a twisted walking cane.

Esta embraced the old man, kissed his hairy lips. The old man smiled.

"Love you, lovely," he said. His voice was low and gravelly. His eyes fell on Clye. "Who's this?"

Clye felt his chest tighten—his cheeks redden. He straightened and tried to look friendly.

"This is Clye," Esta said. "I'm gonna train him to be a cowboy."

The old man nodded, then hobbled forward with his cane. He extended his hand to Clye. "Jerimiah Galthor."

Clye shook Jerimiah's wrinkled hand, nodded. "Clye Galler."

"Glad to have you here, son," Jerimiah smiled.

Esta patted her husband on the back. "Let's go in for supper." She looked up at Clye. "You too."

The night was quiet at the ranch.

THE WENKIID CIRCLED Clye, clucking its forked

tongue and rattling the frills that framed its head like a great green mane. Clye kept his grip on the lasso, resisted the urge to whip out his pistol.

Esta stood just outside the fence, finishing a bowl of porridge Jerimiah had boiled for breakfast. She had taught Clye how to use a lasso earlier that morning, and now he was in the pen with a wenkiid.

The beast circled still, cocking its beaked head at the newcomer. The lizard-like creature flicked its long tail as it moved, the arch of its scaly back eye-height to Clye. It pawed the sand with its four long, hardy limbs, each equipped with hard, hooflike nails at the end of the scaly green fingers. The end of its tail was covered with soft, almost featherlike spines.

Clye tried to keep his hands from shaking, praying that the wenkiid had eaten recently. He recalled what Esta had told him about breaking wenkiids. "You get the lasso over their head and don't let go. They settle down real easy after that."

Slowly, he swirled the loop of the lasso as Esta showed him earlier—down at his side, up over his head, fingers loosely gripping the knot.

The wenkiid flared its green frills and pawed the ground with its hooves.

Clye bit his lip. He swung the lasso around quicker. He felt the tug of the rope beginning to pull out of his hand and released it toward the circling wenkiid.

The rope hit the sand, and the beast leaped into the air, cawing. Clye gathered up the rope, positioned his hands to throw again, but the wenkiid had changed its mood. It cawed and charged toward Clye, frills out, head down. Clye turned tail and ran toward the fence. Esta was laughing, but the wenkiid still charged.

Clye tripped in the dust and fell face-first in the sand, dropping the rope. The wenkiid jumped on top of him. Clye rolled onto his back, suddenly pinned by the creature's hooves pressing into his side. The wenkiid bent its neck and peered down at him, the black eyes staring into his own. The gray beak opened, and Clye dodged. The wenkiid struck the dust beside Clye's head so close, Clye could feel its breath as it exhaled and drew back for another blow. Clye felt for the pistol at his side, yanked it out and fired at the sand.

The wenkiid screamed and jumped off Clye. Clye leaped to his feet, scooped up the lasso with his free hand. The wenkiid rattled its frills and began circling. Clye shoved his pistol back into its holster, then swung the lasso around his head. The wenkiid narrowed its eyes, Clye narrowed his own.

A subtle tug of the rope, and Clye released the lasso. It shot out like a snake toward the wenkiid, the loop winding around its head. Clye yanked it taut. The creature thrashed, and Clye held onto the rope, teeth gritted. The wenkiid let out a strangled caw and stopped struggling.

Clye walked toward the creature, winding the rope as he walked to keep it tight. He approached the wenkiid, breathing hard. The animal eyed him and clucked its tongue. Clye very gently brushed its scaly frills. The wenkiid went silent.

Rope still in hand, Clye scrambled onto the animal's back. The wenkiid cawed, bucked and kicked.

"Shh… Shh... It's okay, girl, it's okay. Yeah, that's it." Clye held on with his knees, looping the rope around his arm. He reached forward and grabbed a pair of soft frills at the base of the neck. He tapped the creature's side with his snake-embossed boots.

The wenkiid trotted forward, shaking its head every few steps. Clye kept his voice low, kept reassuring it. He led the beast up to the fence where Esta stood.

The old cowboy smiled, tipped her hat. "Good job," she said. "You're a natural."

Clye grinned, chest still heaving.

Jeremiah hobbled out of the ranch house, one hand holding something tucked inside his blue jacket. When he approached, he pulled the thing out and handed it to Esta: a cowboy hat as dusty and red as the sandstone in Coiter Mine. Esta smiled, handed her husband the empty porridge bowl, which he took with a bow. She looked up at Clye.

"I think you've earned this," she said, holding up the hat.

Clye's chest tightened. A cowboy hat. Respect. Again. Clye leaned down and took the hat, placed it on his head. It felt right—felt as if it was made for him. It was good to know that something was made for him in a world where even the sand could kill. It gave a man a feeling of destiny.

Esta eyed him from under her brown hat. "What are you thinkin', boy?"

Clye snapped to. "Nothin'—I'm glad to be here. You say I'm a cowboy?"

Esta wrinkled her nose, shook her head. "No, not yet, you ain't."

Jeremiah smiled, still holding the porridge bowl in one hand. "Least not till after lunch."

A FEW HOURS LATER they sat down to a lunch of nawfa steak boiled with green leeks. While they were all around the table, Esta got up and brought in an ammo pouch filled with bullets. She gave it to Clye.

Afterward, the threesome sat on the porch, watching the wind blow the sand across the desert that separated their haven from the town of Jute. The ranch house sat like a mother hen tucked in a nest of boulders, the barns like chicks dotting the sand to the east of the house. Esta and Jerimiah sat in their rocking chairs, while Clye sat on the top step of the porch, hugging his knees to his chest. Jerimiah had his face behind the weekly *Jute Chronicle*.

"Hmm." Esta's rocking chair creaked as she moved it. "Clye, your family take good care of ya?"

The sand danced silently across the desert plain. Clye shrugged. "Mostly."

Esta rocked her chair harder. "Clye, you're lookin' fer somethin'," she said.

Clye's throat tightened. He pulled his hat down lower.

"I ain't never seen an outlaw rushin' around to do good like you do."

*I gotta free myself from my past*, Clye thought, but he did not say it.

"I wanna teach you the Way of Sand."

Clye turned around. He cocked an eyebrow. "I already know it—better 'an most. You saw me lift the sandstone."

Esta stopped rocking her chair, eyed the young man. "Are you addicted, though?"

Clye remembered the white western grains in his pocket. He could almost feel them on his tongue. "No," he said. "I mean, I don't take 'em often. It ain't a habit." He coughed.

Esta smiled. "Grains catch ya. Can't escape it, that's just

what happens when you use 'em over and over. The feeling they give is very nice, eh?"

Clye wrinkled his nose. "What are you trying to say?"

"Grains won't fill it, son," Esta said, her smile fading, her voice becoming grave. "Neither will family, neither will name."

Clye clenched his teeth at the word 'family.' He looked up at Esta. "'Only the Sandwalker,' eh?"

Esta pursed her lips, nodded.

"I pray every night—I don't know if he hears. It was an awful long time ago he left Drode, right? I don't know. I'm doing what I can." Clye shook his head. "But it doesn't fix it—doesn't fix my past." He thumped his chest. "Doin' the best I can, I tell you."

Esta shook her head. "That ain't what I mean. If I take ya out to the Living Sands—"

"Well look at that! Justin Croy escaped Jute prison!" Jerimiah bobbed up from his paper

"Kein!" Clye spat.

Esta looked over at her husband's paper. "When this happen?"

"Last night," Jerimiah said, scratching his beard. He frowned over the paper again. "Says they think a couple outlaws barged in and shot up the Sheriff. Mm. Poor man. Rest in peace. The lawmen came when they heard the gunshot, but Justin and the others were already out of town. Surprised we didn't hear their ruckus." Jerimiah closed the paper, shook his head. "Shameful. That sheriff was a good man."

Clye pursed his lips. He looked down at the scar on his thumb.

"What's the town doin' about it?" Esta asked.

"High alert," Jerimiah said. "They're keepin' it locked

down while they mourn the sheriff. Justin's price went up, but no one's out lookin' for 'im."

Esta frowned. "They probably moved their hideout."

Clye nodded, eyes still studying his scar. "Always. That's the outlaw way."

Esta rose from her rocking chair. "Well, Mr. Outlaw, you wanna wrangle another wenkiid?"

Clye winced, then nodded slowly. He rose to his feet and looked up at Esta's wrinkled face. Her dark eyes pierced soul and shadow.

Clye adjusted his cowboy hat. "Yes, ma'am."

## TWELVE
# KIVES

CLYE RODE THE imbval through the open doors of one of Esta's barns. He trotted into the dim interior, taking the imbval into a stall and sliding off the saddle. The creature lifted up its horned head and grunted.

"Shh... Shh... It's okay, girl."

Clye unstrapped the saddle and placed it on the wooden divider that kept the stalls apart. He scratched the imbval's gray fur a moment, then turned and walked out of the stall. Hay was strewn all over the floor, speckled with various shapes and sizes of animal dung. Clye walked out of the barn, closed the great double doors, and locked them.

He glanced at the sky. The sun was setting in the west, bathing the world in a soft pink glow—pink like bloodstains almost washed out.

Clye inhaled, closed his eyes. He'd learned a lot in the last few days—breaking animals, saddling them, cleaning stalls. There'd been a lot of time to think. And think he had.

His pa was dead. It felt like someone had ripped a hole in his chest. He could hide it with work, but he couldn't fill it. His pa gave him something that no one could—not Ma, not Esta and Jerimiah, not prayer, not Hollin's keining job. Paul Galler gave a deep love that was unaffected by action or mood. Now that love was yanked out, leaving that deep hole behind.

Clye exhaled. He could see the tops of Jute's buildings just peeking up over the southern horizon like skeleton fingers. Kobe had gone back to his own ma—a ma he was fiercely protective of, but seemed to not love immensely. Clye wondered what he was up to—if he had applied to be a ranger with the reward money, if his ma helped or loved him at all. Clye's thoughts flashed to his own mother standing silently on the porch in front of her cemetery-clean yard. His heart clenched. Kobe couldn't feel that pain.

Clye turned and felt the rough wooden doors of the stall barn. He undid the lock.

CLYE REIGNED IN the imbval beside Kobe's fence. Night had fallen, but the moon above was bright as Kobe's glowing mushrooms. Clye could see the little cottage in almost perfect detail. Round wooden shingles—most of them cracked—bright blue paint slathered over the rotting cottage siding. An uncovered porch wrapped the front, dipping down into the yard—trying to hide the scorched grass. The yard was hemmed in by a short fence with peeling paint. Lamplight glowed from within the curtained windows. Clye slid off the imbval, wrapped the reigns around a fencepost. The creature whinnied for a moment, but a look from Clye silenced it.

Clye hopped the fence and walked to the house. As he approached, he heard voices coming from inside. Clye pulled his hat down over his eyes, crept up to the porch, and put his ear to the door.

"…you keep 'em or not?" A high, twangy male voice.

Silence.

"We'll search the house. Tie the boy up, he's useless." A shiver went down Clye's spine. The voice of Justin Croy.

Boots scraping, then a gunshot.

Clye whipped out his pistol, found the door unlocked, and yanked it open. The cottage was one large room. Just inside the door stood Justin Croy. Beyond him, two outlaws tangling with an armed Kobe. An old woman sat on a mattress in the corner. Justin stood still with one hand on his hat, the other hand gripping his sword.

Clye raised his pistol to fire at Justin, but found his hands shaking. Justin. Apples. Long nights in the caves reading and imagining adventures. Clye pulled the trigger, missed completely.

Justin jerked around and Clye found the tip of a sword at his throat. Justin smiled.

"Oh. Nice to see you." He turned back to his men who were trying to wrest the pistol from Kobe's hand. "Leave the boy alone. Get the pistol, though." Justin turned back to Clye. "I could slit your throat right now, for putting me in that hole, but I always did like you."

Clye heard Kobe gasp as Justin's two outlaws stepped aside, holding the boy's pistol.

Justin motioned with his sword. "Sit down. Give the old lady some company. You always liked the old ones, I recall."

Clye glared, moved slowly toward the mattress, fist still curled around his pistol. He passed Justin's two outlaws, grabbed the hand of Kobe, who was sitting on the floor.

The boy's eyes were watering, hands trembling. Clye hefted Kobe to his feet, scowling at the outlaws, finger on the trigger of his pistol.

Justin waved his sword. "Keep walking," he grunted, eyes narrowed.

Clye nodded. He walked Kobe over to the mattress beside his old mother. Clye sat down on the edge of the mattress.

Justin strode up, both hands on his sword now pointed at the floorboards. He looked over at his two outlaws. "What are we going to do?" he said.

One of the outlaws nodded, fingered Kobe's revolver. "Kill the witnesses, get the money?"

Justin wrinkled his nose. "That won't do. Not since this *Yeller* showed up." He flicked out his sword, held it inches from Clye's face.

Clye's finger rested on the trigger of his revolver. "You know I could drop all three of you right now."

Justin smiled. "I know. But you won't. Just like I won't slit your smug little throat."

Clye bit his lip.

Justin sheathed his sword, pursed his lips. His gaze swept the floor, the walls, the ceiling, gaze darkening with each new thing it took in.

"Kein!" he kicked at the dust on the floorboards. "Thought I'd get away with it!"

Clye eyed his old friend, studying the sag of his shoulders, the way his breath rasped when he was angry. *What did he do?* Clye thought.

Justin straightened, turned to his men.

"Game's off. We're already losing time. We gotta leave for

Annaday in an hour. Proyton wants us to pick up something."
He spun to face Clye. "What do you say, Lyle? Be back at
Coiter Mine in three days or your mother dies."

Clye jumped to his feet, felt the sword-point against his
neck. He glared at Justin. "What the hona does my ma have to
do with anything?"

Justin smiled. "'Ma'. Cute."

"Shut up," Clye snapped. "Why Coiter?"

"'Cause Proyton isn't afraid," Justin scowled. "Your ma
will be there, and you'll do what Dayer Proyton asks of you. I
think he has words for both you and your old lady."

"You're bluffing," Clye hissed. "It takes three days to get
to Annaday, another three back to Jute, and another one and a
half to the mine."

Justin nodded. "Glad to see you know your numbers.

Clye wrinkled his nose. "Not even a wenkiid goes that fast."

"Maybe you just don't ride 'em right." Justin frowned. "But
know this—your ma *will* be at Coiter mine in three days, and
she *will* die if you're not there. I *can't* explain." He turned to
his men. "Out, boys, we've delayed long enough."

The two outlaws shrugged and rushed out of the house.
Justin stayed a moment, one hand holding the tip of his hat,
one hand holding his sword to Clye's throat. His gaze flicked
to the gun in Clye's hand. "Now, Clye, I want you to drop
that gun."

Clye gripped the pistol tighter. "I thought you were sure I
wouldn't shoot you."

Justin chuckled. He licked his lips. "I also remember what it
felt like when you sent a piece of lead up my arm."

Clye squared his shoulders. He flicked a glance at Kobe and

his mother before he spoke. "I'm glad you remember. It's a rare thing to see Justin Croy afraid."

Justin shook his head, flashed a fierce smile. "Always hated guns."

"Used 'em plenty in the mine."

"Before you and that little *kive* shot me." Justin glared at Kobe with fury in his eyes. He turned back to Clye, his hand shaking, sword-tip dancing inches from Clye's throat. "Bring that hona-damned kive with you to the mine—my request."

Clye shook his head. "I'm not sacrificing a kid."

Justin drew in a breath through clenched teeth. "Murderous kid."

Clye felt heat rise in his chest. "Ain't right to take it out on Kobe—it was your cousin who shot your ma in cold blood, not he."

"Don't talk about family in front of these...kives!" Justin jabbed his sword forward, slicing a short cut into the side of Clye's neck.

Clye pulled back, falling against the mattress. Justin spun on his heels and fled the house. Clye fired once, but hardly aimed. The bullet shattered one of the windows.

Clye covered his bleeding neck with his hand. He could feel the blood slowing. He turned to Kobe. The boy looked up at him with jaw set, eyebrows narrowed.

"We're comin' wif ya," he said.

"No—he'll kill you," Clye shook his head. "I'll take you to Esta's ranch. You'll be safe there."

Kobe's old mother raised her wrinkled hand. "We ought to take the money with us."

Kobe patted her shoulder, nodded. "Oy, Marm."

He hopped off the mattress. He tugged up the sheet corner, reached in, and pulled out a bag that clinked with coins. He handed it to his mother and looked up at Clye.

"Let's be goin'," he said. "We don't have much toime."

Clye holstered his pistol, keeping his other hand tight against his neck. He awkwardly helped Kobe's Ma to her feet.

His stomach sank. More people to endanger on a mission against that horrible Justin Croy.

Kobe and his ma would be safe at the ranch—then all Clye would have to worry about was *his* mother. His mother—angry, sad old woman—could die in three days. He didn't want to think about it, but his mind wandered unbidden.

His ma—dead in the dark of the mine at the hands of Justin Croy. She could never love him then—never climb out of her mourning dress and rejoice in the fact that her son had cleared his name.

# THIRTEEN

# BE CLEANSED

A DAY TILL they had to be at the mine. Clye sat on the steps of Esta's porch, head in his hands. The sun shone down from the rising east, casting the house's shadow over Clye and the sand at his feet. He removed his hat, fiddled with the brim. He looked out across the sand toward Jute, watching the tumble-weeds bounce in the breeze.

Town full of people, full of religion, full of beggars, full of outlaws, full of lawmen, full of death. Clye shook his head. He bent the sandstone-red hat brim back and forth in his hands.

Kobe and his mother had settled in immediately. Kobe's mother stayed very quiet, always holding the money-sack. Jerimiah lent Kobe one of his pistols, which Kobe practiced with for much of the day. The boy seemed determined to go with Clye to the mine. It was certain death—why was the kid so set to take the risk? Perhaps he wanted revenge, perhaps he was craving more adventure. Perhaps both.

The door creaked open. Clye quickly donned his hat. He listened to the boot-steps—watched Esta's tall leather boots march down the steps till she was sitting beside him.

She looked off into the distance, the breeze blowing the fly-aways from the bun that sat just under her hat. Clye hadn't realized how deep the wrinkles under her eyes really were. The old lady looked very tired all of a sudden.

"Tough one," she said.

Clye nodded. He dug the toe of his boot into the sand at the foot of the steps. "Esta," he said, quiet, "have you ever sinned?"

"Kein, yes!" Esta chuckled. Then she frowned, shook her head. "I was *not* the good little girl my ma and pa wanted. I was rebellious, drunk, runnin' away from anything that smelled human."

Clye nodded, rubbed the scab on his neck. "I understand the feelin'."

Esta looked off in the distance, a little moisture coming into her eyes. "Anything that smelled human," she repeated. "I was more animal than anything, Clye. I'd be dead on the mountains where the skeletons wake themselves if it weren't for..." She paused, chewed on her lip. "Yeah. Then *he* found me."

"Sandwalker," Clye stiffened.

Esta smiled. "Yeah. First him, then Jerimiah. Kein, he was a handsome kive! And just what I needed."

Esta adjusted her position and looked Clye right in the eyes. "Clye, you can't fix yourself. No one can—I certainly couldn't! I'm tellin' ya—only the Sandwalker can fill that hole in your heart, make you truly clean." She put a hand on his shoulder. "Do you want to taste the Living Sands?"

Clye bit his lip. He looked off toward Jute, watched the breeze whipping the dust off the desert floor into little clouds—burdens to be hauled across the desert by the wind.

*Burden*. That's what Clye carried with him. It had felt like a massive weight on his shoulders—the years of living as an outlaw, stealing, killing, bringing shame to his family's name. That burden had not been something that added to him—it had been something that took away, that stole from who he truly was. A hole—massive, living, consuming.

Saving his ma with that hole in him would only consume her as well. Vanquishing Justin Croy with that hole in him would only lead to more killing, more death. Hona, would he always be an outlaw?

Clye turned to Esta but found it hard to stare into her eyes. He dropped his gaze. "Show me the Sands."

ESTA AND CLYE mounted steeds and took off at a trot from the ranch. Esta led the way northeast, deeper into the desert. The sand hissed like fleeing snakes under the claws of their cathrahds, the wind blowing dust against the animals.

Clye pulled his hat down to shade his eyes, squinted out at the landscape. Mountains rose high in the north, dunes beneath them. Nearer than the dunes stretched the flat plain of sand which was only broken occasionally by rocks and bones. The dead desert. Hungry, deadly, consuming all of Drode, as the myths tell.

The sky bent down above them, digging into the horizon with sharp, blue claws. Clye wondered why the sky held so tightly to its horizon, yielding ground reluctantly as you came toward it, ever fleeing but unable to let go of what held it down.

Clye watched the sand rolling beneath the feet of their mounts, noticing the subtle changes in color and texture of the sand grains. He looked up at Esta who rode her cathrahd slowly ahead, surveying the sands below her.

"Esta," he called, "are the Sands in a hidden place?"

"No," she answered, without looking back, "the Sands are blown by the wind all through the desert. Mixed in with so many other grains you'd never notice. We're goin' to the source—least, the only source I've found."

"Anyone else find it—or just you?"

"Don't know." Esta straightened in her saddle.

Clye fell silent. He glanced at the mountains standing in the distance. Tomorrow his mother would be in a mine in those mountains. Mercy, she seemed to hate him when he wept over Pa's grave! Clye shook his head, tried to keep the burning tears back, turned his gaze back to the sky. He couldn't blame her. He'd been a terrible son. Throwing away their quaint little life of church and gardening for outlawry. Almost ten years away from home, ten years wanted dead or alive.

It was another hour or two of silent desert trekking before Esta stopped and dismounted. Clye was hungry, but he said nothing as he slid off his cathrahd and walked up to Esta.

She stood facing a small dune that rose eight or ten feet from the desert floor, flecked with dark brown sand.

Clye's heartbeat quickened. "These the Sands?" he pointed to the dune.

"Over it," Esta returned. She spun around, smiled, bunching up the wrinkles around her eyes. "You go on alone. I'll wait here."

Clye nodded, took a deep breath, and stepped toward the dune.

"Oh. And you should probably leave your boots here."

Clye stopped, turned to face Esta. "My boots?"

Esta smiled and shrugged. "It's just how it works."

"Take my boots off?" Clye frowned. He shook his head. "No. Nobody's that stupid. In less than an hour I'll be dead—boiled from the inside out."

"I'm alive, ain't I?" Esta clacked the heels of her boots together. "It's what He wants—it's trust."

"Mm-mm. Kein no." Clye stared down at his own boots, noticing that awful serpent pattern etched into the leather.

He felt dirty, suddenly. It was not a new feeling—he'd carried it with him for years, kept it mostly dormant. But here it flared up again—filth. Dirt. He wanted to throw off those boots and the blood-red jacket and rush over the dune and find his freedom—find his worth—find the strength to defeat the outlaw within and the outlaw holding his mother captive.

What was Clye Galler made of? Outlaw dirt, or living sand?

Clye sat down on the sand, felt how hot it was in the afternoon sun. He yanked his boots off, exposed his pale, wrinkled toes to the open air for the first time in years. He felt the sand against his bare heel, could sense the blood rushing, heating within him. Clye glanced up at Esta, set his jaw.

She smiled.

Clye jumped to his feet, ripped off his jacket, and rushed up over the dune. Cresting it, he saw below him a vast, circular expanse of dark brown sand. It almost looked like a huge shadow had been cast on the desert floor. But though it was darker than the rest of the sand, Clye sensed something like light emanating from it. Not visible—but light nonetheless. The hairs on the back of Clye's neck tingled as he looked at the sand—a gentle brushing, a beckoning.

He slid down the dune, sweat pouring down his face. His feet felt like they were made of fire. Clye rushed out onto the dark sand, tripped, and fell flat on his face, hat tumbling away.

Heat consumed him. Clye shook, every muscle screaming, but he couldn't rise. The sand had claimed him—the feet, the face were all it needed. No salra or jacket sleeves could protect him now. He would die in a matter of seconds.

"Sandwalker save me," he whispered into the grains beneath him.

Clye inhaled, felt the sand go up his nose. Instantly, a cooling sensation washed over him. His limbs stopped trembling. His face stopped sweating.

Clye tried to rise, but he couldn't. All he could do was lift his head, bring his gaze barely off the ground. With his limited vision, the dark sand seemed to stretch on forever in all directions. Like with inhaling any sand, Clye could *feel* all the sand around him—each grain connected to every other—in his mind, in his fingertips. But the sand was not at his command. It seemed *happy* that he was there, but not as a dog or a slave might. It was like a friend—the sand was a vast connected family of which he was just one grain. One grain in thousands. Together. One. Alive and happy.

Clye smiled. He felt peace here. But heaviness. He shut his eyes. The filthiness that he'd felt earlier came back, collecting as a great weight on his chest. It grew heavier. Every passing second, more and more weight on his chest. Each time the weight increased, he could sense what it was. Hatred. Rebellion. Loneliness. Fear. Each little weight had a name—a name he'd never thought to assign. Hona, he felt so heavy.

Clye pressed his face into the sand, almost pulled by the great weight on his chest. "Cleanse me, clean me," he gasped, inhaling more sand, "I'm so sorry for all this. All this. Please. Please cleanse me."

Footsteps. Hushed, far away, slow but even. Steady, coming nearer. Clye heard them stop just inches from his face.

He opened his eyes and saw two bare feet beneath an old pale robe like the ministers wore. He could feel kindness, *goodness* like his pa had or some of the ministers seemed to have. Clye wanted to get away, wanted to run. The goodness of this person was so strong that it etched all his badness into sharp shadows.

Suddenly, a whisper. Was it coming from the ground, from the wind, from the man standing before him? Clye didn't know, but he heard the words, soft, simple: "Be cleansed."

Clye shut his eyes, felt tears spring into them. The weight on his chest melted into the dark sand below him, and the hole it left felt like it was being filled with cool water.

"Thank you," he murmured, face buried into the sand, tears soaking the ground.

Clye felt his hat being placed back on his head.

Footsteps. Slowly growing softer, vanishing into the distance. Heat returning.

Clye got to his feet, the heat scalding his feet minor in comparison to the overwhelming coolness that held his heart. In the distance—bare feet moving at an easy pace but robe flapping as if the man was running with the swiftness of a wen-kiid—walked a man in the tattered robe and breeches of an older time, his hair blowing free and uncovered in the wind.

# FOURTEEN

# I HATE YOU

BY THE WEST SIDE of the ranch house, Clye tightened the saddle around the wenkiid's belly. What would take an easy day and a half by cathrahd or imbval would take a hard half-day riding a wenkiid. But a seven-day roundabout in under three days—Justin must be feeding his wenkiids grains or cigars or *something* to make them go that fast.

Clye scratched the creature behind the neck, smiled when it gargled with pleasure.

He adjusted his hat and looked back to Esta and Kobe saddling the other wenkiid. Kobe had never ridden one, so Esta thought it best to have him ride with her. Clye had not been able to convince Kobe to say behind. Kobe's mother and Jerimiah stood on the corner of the porch, quiet, hands clasped.

Clye turned back to the beast, hopped up on the saddle, and took the reins. The lasso tied to his belt flopped against his thigh.

Hona, last night had been wonderful! Clye felt ten pounds lighter and two inches taller. He knew they would be in for it in the mine, but he felt ready. He'd save his ma. If he couldn't save her—kein, he couldn't think about that now. The pain of Pa's death still weighed on him. Not a gnawing hole, but a blunt pain, throbbing slowly in the depths of his veins.

Clye glanced back to see if Esta and Kobe had mounted their wenkiid. They had—Kobe straight-backed, fists clenched like he was holding a pistol in each. Esta's hat swooped down over her face, hiding all but her bright-toothed smile.

"You'll come back with a ma, Clye," she said. "Or if not, I can be your ma."

Clye smiled, though the thought of losing his ma stung him. Before he could answer, Kobe piped up, glaring up at the back of Esta's head. "Meant *maha*, roight? Moiner slang for woife."

"What the hona?" Clye's jaw went slack. "She's married, Kobe!"

"*Maha, maha,*" Esta sang.

Clye put his hand to his forehead. "Let's move out before someone says something else stupid." He inhaled. "Onward, posse!" His voice rang off the rocks and desert sand.

He spurred the wenkiid, and the reptile shot off north, toward the sand and the dunes and the jagged mountains. The wind gushed in Clye's face, whipping the jacket around his shoulders and nearly taking the hat from his head. Clye clamped the hat down as the wenkiid sped forward. Clye chanced a half-glance behind him.

Esta and Kobe barreled toward him on their wenkiid, the wind changing their jackets into flapping capes about their shoulders. Farther behind, the ranch was growing steadily smaller. Ahead, the mountains waited for them on the horizon.

Clye smiled. What a thrill to be going so fast. He'd never ridden a wenkiid until he broke this one a few days ago. He wondered how Esta had managed to capture them.

THE SUN HAD reached the middle of the sky and begun its long descent into the west. Ahead, Clye could see the ruddy sandstone of Mount Shonwick jutting out from the range, Co-iter's black mouth opening at its base.

Clye was about to face Justin again—his friend, holding his ma captive. Clye shook his head, turned his attention back to the gaping mouth of Coiter Mine.

"We gotta be careful!" he shouted to the posse, voice swallowed up by the wind. "Keep your weapons handy!"

They had just passed the dune fields, leaving a straight shot of flat sand separating them from Coiter mine. Clye thought he could see some figures standing in the mine entrance. The guards, possibly, unless Proyton Gang had fully quit secrecy and had killed the guards and replaced them with their own. Proyton had already abandoned the outlaw way in refusing to move their hideout—killing the miners and blowing their cover was not unthinkable.

Wind began to gush across the plain, throwing sand at Clye and the others. Clye squinted to be able to see, kept his hand firmly on his hat. The angle of the wind felt unnatural to him. He looked at the mine entrance. Sand was swirling in a whirl-wind in front of it, growing thicker by the moment till the guards were completely obscured.

Clye reined in his wenkiid. The sandstorm was growing—even now heavy splashes of sand were pummeling him. He could no longer see the mine—all was roiling sand between them and Coiter. Esta and Kobe halted their wenkiid beside his.

"Nice manners!" Clye snapped. "Justin invites us here just to keep us out."

A spray of sand washed over the posse.

Esta shielded her eyes with her hands. "I can try to reverse the storm while you two run in!"

"Forget it! This is *Justin Croy* we're dealin' with!" Clye could barely keep his eyes open now. Sand engulfed him. *Sandwalker help us.*

His wenkiid clicked uneasily.

"Shh... Shh..." Clye scratched the creature's frills, turned to Esta, forcing his eyes open by slits. "We're goin' in!" he shouted.

Esta nodded. Kobe kept his head down.

Clye spurred his wenkiid, and the creature gasped, diving deeper into the sandstorm.

Sand. Crashing into his ears, wriggling into his eyes, sliding up his nose. Everywhere—every bit of him that was exposed was attacked by bone-dry armies of sand. Clye shut his eyes and kept his head down. He felt his temperature rise. He held his breath, unable to draw anything but sand into his mouth. His ears were assaulted with the roar of the storm. Then Clye heard galloping, roaring, thumping that shook the very ground beneath the wenkiid's hooves. The sand began to swirl slower—still thick, but slower.

Clye coughed, trying to expel the sand from his lungs in order to take another breath. First inhale—failure. Sand shot up his nose, inducing the heightened senses that come with grains. But it made it no better—he only felt more strongly the tightness in his lungs and the desperation for air in his racing mind.

The waves of sand crashed against him less harshly, sand about him swirling still more slowly. Lungs burning, Clye gasped in a breath. Only a few grains entered his mouth; the rest—pure air. Clye gradually opened his eyes, realized he was barreling toward the two men standing in the mine entrance. Clye reined in his wenkiid.

"Oy! Who be entrancing here?" shouted one of the men, face hidden by a wide ranger's hat. He and his fellow stood beside the now-dilapidated wooden desk in the corner of the mine entrance.

"Who be entrancing here?" repeated the Ranger.

Kobe and Esta brought their wenkiid to a halt beside Clye's.

"*Entrancing?*" Kobe snorted, then fell into a fit of coughing.

Kobe slid off the wenkiid, began walking toward the men in the mouth of Coiter Mine.

Clye slid off his own beast and drew his pistol.

Kobe put his hands on his hips. "That's an awful farce of a moiner's accent, zurrah."

Ranger spit in the sand. "Kein you, lad." He turned to his partner. "Let's go. Justin's waiting."

The two outlaws spun around and bolted into the mine.

"Hey! Where's my ma?" Clye shouted, but they kept running.

Clye glanced at Kobe and Esta, who had also slid off her wenkiid. "Wait—get back on—we've gotta get after 'em!"

Esta shook her head. "Wenkiids slow down in the dark. They'd think it were nighttime and fall fast asleep."

"Kein!" Clye looked back into the gaping skull's mouth of Coiter mine. He inhaled. "After 'em, boys!"

"Lady," Esta corrected.

Clye rushed into the mine, each footstep echoing through the spacious tunnel. Kobe nimbly caught up to and passed him. Ahead, Clye could see the two outlaws running, approaching the swinging rope bridge. The kives had a good head start. Clye narrowed his eyes. He could catch them.

Not before Kobe, but he could catch them.

Clye watched the outlaws speed across the rope bridge and quickened his pace. Oddly, there were no sounds of hammers or any other work. The mine was empty as a living man's tomb.

Kobe seemed to float across the bridge after the men. Clye followed, stomach churning as the bridge creaked and swayed with every step. The outlaws hustled around a large cathrahd and ran along a ledge on the left-hand wall. Kobe ran after them.

Clye slowed his pace. The beast stood on the edge of a gaping hole in the mine floor, harnessed to a cart. Its spiny armored back looked gray in the dim light of the mine. The cliff's edge cut through the darkness, joining up with the ledge on the left-hand wall. The cathrahd had no saddle—the miners likely walked alongside it in the dark, tugging at the leather harness. It was certainly broken, but saddle-less and rein-less. Clye approached the lump of a creature, yanking out his lasso and twirling it slowly.

He felt the rope tug in his grasp and released it to fly like a sparrow through the air, looping around the creature's neck.

Clye walked up to the cathrahd, winding the rope around his arm. The animal did nothing but paw the sandstone floor with its scaly claws. Putting the lasso in his mouth, Clye clambered up onto the creature's back, fitting his fingers between the large bony plates that covered the cathrahd.

Now astride, Clye looked around. Esta had passed him and caught up to Kobe. The two pelted down the ledge toward the fleeing outlaws.

Clye loosened the lasso's grip around the cathrahd's neck, then gripped the loop of the rope like makeshift reins, the tail of the lasso still in Clye's mouth. He spit it out, letting it dangle in his lap.

"Come on, boy!" he said, clicking his tongue.

The beast moaned, inched forward. *Hona—gotta go faster*. Clye steered it left, toward the ledge, then thrust his spurs into the creature's side. A yelp, and it charged forward, stampeding down the ledge at an alarming rate. Clye held onto the loop of his rope, making quick turns to keep the cathrahd from speeding off the narrow stone ledge.

It was growing darker in the mine. Clye prayed the narrow ledge would widen before all visibility was lost.

He was approaching Kobe and Esta. Clye could just see them, hustling down to where the ledge indeed widened and joined up with the rest of the mine floor.

"Watch out!" Clye screamed.

Esta and Kobe turned their heads, froze momentarily, then spun around and ran from him like mice from a gunshot.

Clye bit his lip, steering the beast closer to the wall. He narrowly missed crushing his friends.

It was too dark now to see anything beyond vague shapes in the shadows. Clye thought he could see two human shapes running down the broad slope of the mine. He spurred his beast on faster. It was surprising the outlaws didn't rush off into one of the side tunnels or disappear into one of the vertical shafts in the floor. Clye frowned, the cold mine air rushing in his face.

"Trap," he muttered. From the beginning the whole thing had been a trap—bring Lyle Yeller in and kill him, or make him join Proyton gang. But there was a chance he could barter for his mother's life, if the kives had actually brought her.

Now that he thought of it, that wasn't likely. His mother wasn't in the mine—they had lured him in with a lie. Yet Justin Croy had never been one to break his word—he had too much pride for that.

Clye shook his head. If his ma was here, he had to save her. And if she wasn't there, Clye would go down fighting Justin Croy and his master Dayer Proyton.

Clye rushed on, the heavy footsteps of the beast almost deafening.

IT HAD GROWN so dark Clye couldn't see the lasso he was holding. He heard a shout from ahead and a light suddenly appeared—one of the outlaws had donned a glowing miner's hat. The light began to bob, grow smaller. Running.

Clye spurred the animal on again.

The pursuit continued for what felt like an eternity, the light ahead barely slowing. The outlaws must be smoking something strong to have that kind of speed and endurance. In the distance, beyond the light of the miner's cap, Clye could see an orange glow spreading slowly—like blood soaking into desert sand.

As they got nearer, Clye saw that it was the light of the torches ringed around the black floor of the mine. In the center of the black stone floor stood a small crowd of outlaws holding weapons.

The outlaw wearing the miner's cap vanished into the crowd, and Clye came rushing down the slope into the torchlight.

"Whoa, boy!" he said, reining in the cathrahd.

Clye looked down at the pack of outlaws—seven, he'd guess—all armed and filthy as hogs.

Justin Croy stood in the front of the crowd, several yards from

Clye. One hand gripped the brim of his black fedora, the other, the hilt of his long sword. His leather jacket framed his stained white shirt that pinched his neck with a twice-folded collar.

Beside Justin stood Clye's ma in her mourning dress, veil still draped over her face. *So they did bring her.*

"On time, kept your word, fit into the plan without shaking anything—I'm impressed." Justin said, his face hidden by the brim of his black fedora.

He stepped forward, using his sword like a cane. He looked up at Clye, and now Clye could see the flared nostrils, the curved eyebrows, the subtle smile—Clye knew those signs all too well. He gripped the beast's reins tighter.

"You brought the little kive with you?" Justin kept walking, one hand on his fedora, one hand walking his sword forward like a cane.

Clye narrowed his eyes. He let go of the reins to grab his pistol, but didn't draw it.

Justin stopped in front of the cathrahd, nodded to it, looked back up at Clye. "You're a strong man, Clye. Crack shot, too." Emotion slipped into his voice—the slightest break that only a friend could pick out. "Dayer says we can't have you running around anymore. I talked to him, but…"

Clye yanked his pistol out with a flourish, leveled it at Justin. "You drop that thing and I won't shoot."

Justin stared up at Clye with blue eyes narrowed. "You won't kill me, Clye. You have a bird's heart. I like that about you."

"You're going to kill me, though," Clye bit his lip, averted his gaze.

"Dayer wants me to prove my loyalty."

"He's not here. He's not holding your hand."

Justin threw down his sword. He raised his trembling hand in the air, showing off the little finger that had been cut off at the knuckle. "See this? I swore an *oath*, Clye! I *have* to do as Dayer says! Remember the Old Yeller?"

Clye shuddered. White hair, rotting teeth. The Yeller's Oath had to be sworn with one hand in his horrible mouth, the other on a stone where they cut three slashes in the index finger. If the Old Yeller was angry, bullet to the side. If he saw the Oath broken, bullet through the brains.

"You understand," Justin nodded. He stooped down and picked up his sword again. "So now, Clye—"

"What does this have to do with my ma?"

Justin stiffened. He chewed on his lip a moment, gaze on the ground. Then, slowly, he relaxed—rolled his shoulders back. He tapped the stone floor with his sword. "I had nothing to do with it. Dayer said she had to come. I don't know why. If you wanna know you'll have to take it up with him when you're both in Hona."

Clye trained his pistol on his friend's head, breaths coming in short. "So if you kill me, my ma goes free? You return her back to Annaday where everyone knows her?"

Justin stepped toward the great beast, and rubbed the harness that encased its face. "Kill them both," he whispered, and drove his saber into the beast's neck.

Clye fired as the beast buckled beneath him, flinging his shot wide. He started sliding in the saddle toward Justin, who raised his sword.

Clye dove off the side of the beast as Justin brought down his blow.

"What'd you say, Justin?" someone called.

"Kill them!" Justin cried.

Clye saw one of the outlaws grab his ma and pull out a revolver. Clye fired two shots at him; the outlaw collapsed into the crowd. Two other outlaws stepped forward, raised their guns toward Clye.

"Kein!" he grunted, diving as the bullets exploded toward him. He hit the warm stone, the sensation overtaken by the searing pain of a bullet ripping through his arm. Clye bit his lip, rolled, and scrambled to his feet as another barrage struck the floor where he had been. Clye popped off a shot, unsure if he hit anything. Clye rushed toward his mother, who stood still as a statue in the small crowd. One of the outlaws jumped up and grabbed her, a rifle balanced awkwardly under his left arm.

Clye bit his lip and dove at the outlaw, shoving the rifle-barrel aside. It went off with a loud bang and clattered to the ground.

Clye pushed the man down and turned to his silent mother, wrapping his arms around her. "Ma—"

A searing pain tore through his leg—a cut from a knife, shallow, but burning. Clye pulled his mother away, trying to get his aim on the fallen outlaw now wielding a knife instead of a rifle.

Clye cocked his pistol.

"Stop!" screamed Justin from a few yards away.

Both Clye and the outlaw froze. Clye glanced at Justin, one arm around his mother, his gun still pointed at the fallen outlaw.

"Stop," Justin repeated, striding forward, his sword red with the blood of the beast. He narrowed his eyes at Clye. "By the ancient tradition of Drode, I compel you to engage me in a duel to the death."

Clye saw the fire in Justin's eyes. The hatred and humilia-
tion—the eyes of a snake ready to strike.

The outlaw on the ground leaped to his feet and grabbed
Clye's ma. Clye held tighter to her small, quivering shoulders,
but she pushed on his arm. Clye let go, his stomach sinking.
Her face was unreadable behind her veil.

The outlaw took his ma several yards away, along with Justin's other men, carving a large swath around Clye and Justin.

Clye's Ma clasped her hands together, bowed her veiled
head. Clye felt a chill rush down his spine.

"Let the duel begin!" one of the outlaws shouted.

Instantly, Justin charged, sword poised for a sweeping blow.
He was too close for Clye to dodge. Clye fired his revolver
from the hip as Justin swung his sword. The sword bounced
against the bone of Clye's jaw, and he felt the flesh split open,
welcoming the bloody steel. Clye shoved the sword aside
with his revolver, put his left hand to his jaw. The cut was only
about an inch long, but it gouged down to the bone. Biting his
lip for the pain, Clye glanced at Justin, his pistol raised.

Justin had backed up and doubled over, leaning on his
sword. His free hand gripped his stomach. Blood dripped
slowly from the gun-wound. He looked at Clye, eyes burning
with hatred.

"You shot me," he spat, mouth foaming. "You shot me."

"And I might have to do it again," Clye said, trying to keep
the emotion out of his voice. He glanced over at his mother,
stock-still in her black robes. Out of the seven original outlaws in the crowd, only four remained, making a half-circle
behind his ma. Each gripped a weapon. Each held onto his
mother's dress. Heat flared in Clye's chest.

Justin spoke up. "Why did you shoot me?" he hissed, hob-
bling forward on his bloody sword. It flexed massively as he
leaned on it, the tip broken off. "We're friends...why did you
shoot me?"

Clye felt the hot blood coursing down his jaw and dribbling
off his chin. Pain seared his jawbone. He glanced up the ramp
he had charged down earlier. Esta and Kobe hadn't shown up.
*Thank the Sandwalker.*

"Clye." Justin was coughing now. "Why did you shoot me?
Why did you—"

"I have to get my ma home." Clye glanced at his mother.
Still as dead stone.

Justin looked up at Clye, eyes red-rimmed, hand shaking as
it grasped his sword. "What are you trying to earn? A name,
a mother? You're always trying..." Justin paused. He inhaled
and looked up again. "What did killing me earn for you? I
want to know."

"I didn't kill ya," Clye said.

"You will, though," Justin glared, now only a mere yard away.

Clye glanced at Justin's thin hand gripping the sword hilt.
"Not a *step* closer, Justin Croy!" Clye stepped back. He exhaled, glaring into Justin's fiery eyes. "You take a swipe at me
or my ma and I'll shoot." Clye bit his lip, felt a tear rising in
his eye. "I'll shoot, Justin. I'll shoot you dead."

Justin's lips quivered. He bared his teeth. A horrible darkness came into the edge of his blue eyes. "I hate you," he
whispered, voice low and full of spittle.

"No," Clye's voice broke.

Clye raised his pistol as Justin raised his bent sword. Justin
swung it at his old friend's head.

A single gunshot echoed from the walls, loud yet almost a whisper in the deeps of the mine. Two men had kept their word.

Four gunshots rang out, followed by one scream. Then another four shots rang out, followed by four screams.

# FIFTEEN

# SOMEONE'S GOTTA DIE

THE POSSE RODE back to Esta's ranch like death was breathing down their necks. Clye was alone when Esta and Kobe had found him. The bullet-wound in his arm was shallow—Esta was able to pick out the lead and wrap it up by tearing off the hem of her shirt. The sword-wound hurt like hona but the bleeding was slowing. Clye kept his hand on it. He barely talked through the long walk out of the mine and the furious wenkiid ride to the ranch.

The sun was leaning toward the west when they dismounted in front of the porch. They found Jerimiah leaning on the railing, squinting toward the south.

"What's wrong, Jerimiah?" Esta said, rushing up the steps to her husband.

Clye turned his gaze to where the old man was looking. The town of Jute was engulfed in a roiling mass of sand. The sandstorm appeared to be made of several small cyclones—each veiling some corner of the town, sometimes dying down as another storm rose up.

"Proyton," Jerimiah said, shaking. "Kein those outlaws!

They're sacking the town."

Clye's chest sank. All those people—blacksmiths, ministers, beggars, lawmen, kives like Hollin Wesner—at the mercy of Proyton gang.

Clye was so tired, and he hardly knew how to think—his ma lay dead in the bottom of Coiter Mine. Dead at the hands of Proyton gang. He inhaled.

"I'm gonna go," Clye said, flexing his arms. He winced as he felt the pain in his left bicep from the bullet wound. Clye bit his lip. He'd manage. He turned to the porch, looked up at Jerimiah, and stopped.

Jerimiah's bright eyes like stars glinted out beneath the night sky of his thick eyebrows. His hairy lips were pursed, Clye could almost see the teeth clenched behind them. Moisture collected in the wrinkles beneath the old man's eyes. He glanced down at Clye.

"Go, son," he said. "I'm too old to fight."

"Not too old for me," snorted Esta, putting an arm around her husband.

Kobe stood on the sand beside his wenkiid, curly hair tousled around his head. He stood erect, arms straight, right hand inches from the revolver at his hip.

Clye smiled at Kobe, pain shooting through his jaw as his wound broke open. He winced, gently put a hand to it. It'd scab up again soon enough. "Kobe," Clye breathed, "You wanna stay here with your ma and these old folks, or fight Proyton with me? We'll probably die."

"Savin' yor ma were certain death, and oi'm aloive," Kobe nodded firmly. "Let's off. Oi'm a better shot 'an you, after oll."

"I don't know about that," Clye forced a chuckle. He turned to Esta. "I'll take a wenkiid—get us there faster."

"They're winded," she adjusted her hat.

Clye shrugged, winced again at the movement. "I'll bring it back."

WHEN CLYE AND KOBE approached the town on the back of the wenkiid, they saw several houses churning in the dust, half-ripped apart by the force of the storm. Clye's chest tightened. He'd only known Justin Croy to have such a way with sand. The addiction and experience of whoever was controlling this storm must be at least equal to that of Justin, may the kive rest in peace. Clye felt *very* tired suddenly.

Clye steered the wenkiid down the street that led to the saloon. Sacked or not, that building, with all the brick and pillars, should still be standing. It was—more shingles torn off to continue the endless cycle. Dust swirled through the street, not very thick. Shadows draped many of the buildings—only a couple of hours till sundown.

Clye saw a couple people rushing around near the saloon, some with pitchforks and rifles, others with swords and pistols—outlaws, by the way they ran. A few bodies lined the street.

Clye turned the wenkiid into a dark alley between two wood-and-stone houses. He dismounted with a grunt of pain. Kobe followed, silent, pistol already unholstered.

"Keep behind cover," Clye said, his voice dry—emotionless. "Don't shoot unless shot at. I think…" Clye pulled out his revolver, flipping out the cylinder to find he had only one bullet left. He reached into the ammo sack on his belt and silently thanked Esta, pulling out seven bullets and shoving them into the cylinder.

Snapping the revolver closed, he holstered it, peered at Kobe. "We gotta find the Law—organize some sorta force to drive these kives out." Clye walked up to the mouth of the alley and checked the street. "Stick close. Once we find the Law we can catch the gang leaders—bring this hona to an end."

An old woman wielding a cane absurdly over her head darted into a side-street, bellowing some ancient battle cry. Was it love of Law, or passion for her town that drove her?

"Clear," Clye said, and rushed out.

He zigged up to a water trough in the shade of a demolished general store—awning sagging like a corpse-laden noose. Kobe landed behind a barrel a few feet away.

Clye looked through the dust at the saloon, ducked as an outlaw burst from the batwing doors. He held his breath, waiting a moment. Clye looked up again. The street was clear of all except for bodies and debris. The sandstorm had died down, though Clye could hear the scratch of sand upon siding coming from the street over. A few shouts and gunshots ripped the air.

Nodding to Kobe, Clye rushed across the street to the saloon steps. As he mounted the first one, he froze. The body at the foot of the steps. Clye's pulse quickened. Bushy sideburns, a golden tooth glinting in the waning light, a gray suit with a gold watch hanging out of the pocket. No bowler hat.

Clye stepped down beside the body, knelt in the sand. Four red bullet holes stained the chest; a little blood dribbled from the mouth. Clye's hand inadvertently went to the dead man's face, rather than his pocket. Clye jerked his hand back when he felt breath.

"Hollin?"

One of the eyelids opened, and Hollin's bright little brown eye stared back at Clye. No smile tugged at his lips.

"Hey…" Hollin moaned. "I know you…Mr. Outlaw." A shadow passed over his face. "I tried to kill you, once."

Clye looked down at Hollin's wounds. "You alright? I should get you to a doctor."

"No," Hollin coughed, spattering blood up at Clye's face. He shook his head, closed his eye. "I'm a broken man, Mr. Outlaw. And all my money…kein." A garbled sob rose in his throat. "Money's no good when you're dead."

"You're not dead yet," Clye said. He shoved his good arm beneath Hollin's torso, retreated when he saw the man wince.

"It's over," Hollin coughed, sending a fresh spray of blood at Clye's face. "Proyton wins, death wins, and I go to Hona for the sinner I am—I always was." Cracked, bloody lips curled up in a smile. "Embrace your past, eh? Embrace the outlaw you are? I did, and it's too keining late."

"No, no," said Clye, surprised at the tears that rose in his eyes at Hollin's words. He thought he hated Hollin. "It's not too late," Clye said.

Hollin opened both his eyes, smile still there. "The church is a mile away. I won't make it if I wanted to."

"No—I, uh…" Clye fought for words, dug back to his conversations with Esta and the wonder of meeting the Sandwalker on the Living Sands. "The Sandwalker doesn't give a kein about your past or name," he said, "and he's the only thing that can fill the hole in your heart."

"Four holes," Hollin said, gaze drifting to his own chest. He never looked up.

CLYE STOOD UP. He turned his face away from the broken body of his friend. Hollin had never been a true friend—never cared about anything but money. Hona, the man had tried to kill him!

But now, Clye found hot tears working their way out of his eyes. The hypocrisy of death. How was it that someone hated in life was now precious in death? How was it that if you truly knew someone, good or bad, their death was always a tragedy?

Clye shook his head, wiped the tears from his face. He winced as his fingers touched his jaw. Kobe stood a few yards away, scanning the street, pistol raised. Aside from them the road was empty of life.

Clye looked up the street toward the center of town. A massive dust-cloud was gathering there, swirling, roiling, moving slowly toward them like an igru about to land.

Clye unholstered his revolver, looked at Kobe. "Brace yourself little brother. Go find some cover. We ain't lettin' 'em past!"

"Alroight." Kobe nodded and knelt down behind a crate in front of the saloon.

Clye darted to the other end of the street, hiding behind a barrel on the shadowed porch of the general store. Clye exhaled. He pulled his gun up to eye level with a flourish.

The dust rolled up the street, followed by voices, the sound of hooves, and the heavy scratch of cathrahd feet. Clye fired his revolver in the air.

The voices and hooves stopped almost instantly, but the dust swirled on for a while.

"Proyton Gang!" Clye called. "You ain't leavin' this town until the Law arrives and passes judgment over you. Maybe they'll be merciful."

The dust cleared, revealing a crowd of filthy outlaws in various hats. Several of them rode cathrahds or wenkiids and carried long rifles. Several brandished blood-stained swords.

One outlaw, a short man with a double chin, stepped forward from the crowd. He wore the sweeping hat of a bounty hunter, worn and full of holes like the rotting crown of a still-proud prince. Bandoleers crossed his shirt, red as if he'd been shot in the chest. Pistols were stuffed in his belt like so many scorpion stingers, and a sword curved as a dragon's fang was sheathed at his side.

The outlaw tilted his head up, revealing blue eyes and a broken nose. Graying sideburns clawed the sides of his face, and he grinned a gap-toothed smile.

"Lyle Yeller!" he called, hands on his hips, "Or as your mammy likes to call ya, *'Clye Galler.'*"

Clye's chest tightened. The pistol in his hand suddenly felt limp, powerless against this outlaw who knew him.

The outlaw with the double chin continued. "You're one of those do-good outlaws, ain't ya? Rushin' around, tryin' to right the wrongs you've done once upon a time. If it weren't for that *one* character flaw, I might've let you join my gang." He smiled. "Oh. Where are my manners? I'm Dayer Proyton."

Clye froze under the porch awning. Dayer Proyton, who had convinced Justin Croy to cut his finger off in an oath of loyalty. Justin Croy was not a man easily impressed. This Dayer had to have power. Power with sand, power with people, power with money.

"Quiet one, aren't ya?" Dayer chuckled, drawing his curved sword. He held it up to the fading orange sunlight, and Clye could see the curses hand-etched into the steel, could see the rust marring the edge from too much killing and not enough cleaning. "You in the mood for talkin', or fightin', Mr. Galler?" Dayer said.

"Why'd you capture my ma?" Clye said.

Dayer picked at the rusted sword with his fingernails. "A ma's love is a powerful thing, Mr. Galler."

Clye gripped his pistol tighter. "You know ya could've lied? Could've lured me in by love alone."

Dayer stopped scratching at the sword. He looked up at Clye, his blue eyes narrowed. "I don't *lie*, Mr. Galler. Not anymore. Lies are for the weak, to claw their way—"

"Man of honor, I see," Clye said.

"Honor?" Dayer's knuckles whitened around his sword-hilt. "No, Mr. Galler, I ain't a man of honor. I'm a man of *power*. Power don't need to lie."

"Really?"

Dayer adjusted his hat with his free hand. "How's this, Mr. Galler. We duel it out, and if ya kill me, my gang won't kill ya? That's nice, eh?"

"What if you kill me? Then what happens?" Clye raised an eyebrow. Where was Dayer's profit in this?

Dayer shrugged. "We'll keep movin'. Town to town, till the Law and Congress and skeletons in the mountains bow before Proyton Gang. We turn this world from law and poverty into freedom and prosperity. *That's* what we do when I win, Mr. Galler."

Clye felt a chill run down his spine, but there was no breeze. He stole a glance over at Kobe. The boy still held his pistol, crouched down behind the crate by the saloon. If he stayed hidden he could escape to Esta's ranch on the wenkiid. Kobe and the others could hold out well there if the gang didn't attack the ranch full-force.

Clye inhaled, turned back to Dayer. "Issue the duel. But if it's a sword-fight I need a sword."

Dayer grinned. "Oh, it is a sword-fight. But you use your pistol. How many rounds do you have?"

"Seven," Clye answered without checking.

Dayer nodded. "Good enough. You can use those seven shots, and I can use this sword." He held the sword up, the sunlight glinting off the bone-white steel marred with black curses. "And we can both use sand."

*Kein it!* Clye spat under his breath. *He'll kill me by sand alone.* "I consent."

Dayer nodded, tossed his sword to the ground. He threw his leather jacket off and unstrapped his bandoleers. Clye hopped off the porch and followed suit, throwing down his lasso and his ammo pouch, but keeping his jacket on. Could help against the sword slashes, if the blade was still sharp through all that rust. The wound on his jaw throbbed.

Casting the last pistol from his belt and immediately tightening the girth, Dayer grabbed his sword and took a step toward Clye, sword extended.

Clye followed the ceremony, stepping forward on the sand and holding his pistol out at full arm's-length.

The waning sunlight etched the two outlaws into long shadows, air silent as a grave except for the grunting of a few of the cathrahds.

Dayer spoke. "Clye Galler, Dayer Proyton challenges you to a duel. No blood, no break, no plea shall stay the weapons we extend to each other. Only death will appease this challenge once accepted. May the blood of the loser be cursed and sink into the fires of Hona, the body never to be buried. You accept?"

Clye inhaled, looked up at the sky blazing a cloudless blue. *Sandwalker...guard my* life... he prayed.

Clye focused his gaze on Dayer. "I accept," he said.

"Let the duel begin," Dayer said, and stepped forward.

Clye brought both hands to his revolver, watching for the moment Dayer's head came into the sights. A shock of sand burst from the ground, so dense it knocked Clye's hands in the air just as he pulled the trigger. The shot sailed into the now-purple sky.

Clye blinked the sand out of his eyes, only to see Dayer mere yards away, charging, sword raised and mouth open in a hungry smile.

Clye darted to the side and tried to aim his pistol at the charging outlaw. Dayer stopped. He turned toward Clye. Clye fired his revolver. Dayer staggered back, clutching his shoulder.

Suddenly the sand beneath Clye's feet shook and flew out from under him, flinging him on his back and burying him in a dusty grave. Clye clawed his way to his feet, now engulfed in a small sandstorm. The wound on his jaw burned. Clye shut his eyes and closed his mouth. *Sandwalker help me.*

He jumped forward, trying to get beyond the storm. The grains struck his skin less forcefully with each step. As he started to open his eyes, the sands shifted and enveloped him again.

Clye cursed mentally. *Stay focused.* He tried to calm his nerves. It was remarkable that Dayer had such control over sand that he could create storms around others without himself as the eye. Clye figured Dayer would creep in close to the sandy winds, drop them, and dive in for the kill. If so, the outlaw was close—maybe only an arm's length away.

Clye's lungs were burning. He exhaled, chanced a wary inhale through his nose. Grains charged into his nostrils, bringing with them the feeling of connection and heightened awareness. Clye coughed some of the sand out, but the feeling remained—not as pleasant as he had remembered it.

But with the primal connection to the sand, Clye could feel Dayer's presence—a black hole on the edge of his awareness—ahead and to the right. Clye whipped out his pistol with a flourish, shot once, twice, three times in the direction of that darkness.

A grunt—almost a scream—guttural, raw, hacking liquid.

Clye felt the sandstorm lift. He opened his eyes, coughed the rest of the sand out of his lungs, felt the tingling connection to the sand begin to fade. Clye didn't dare brush the sand out of his wound.

On the ground in the middle of the street, Dayer clutched his bloody sword to his chest. He rocked back and forth like a child wishing for its mother. Blood coated his mouth, dribbled down his double chin. One side of his face pressed into the sand. Dayer glared up at Clye with one blue eye.

"Ya cain't do this," he spat. "Ya cain't kill me."

Clye glanced at the gang huddled around their steeds. None of them said anything, none of them moved. Clye knelt down before the fallen leader of Proyton Gang.

"It's a duel, Proyton," he said, "someone's gotta die."

Dayer clenched his teeth, and his eyebrow narrowed over his eye. Clye saw hatred and fear swirling together in the dark pupil.

Dayer hugged his chest tighter, pressing the sword firm

against his sternum. He heaved in a breath—ragged, followed by coughs spattering blood.

"Kein this cruel world," Dayer said, and the life left his eyes.

Clye rose, looked over at Kobe. The boy slowly stood up from behind his crate, motioned with his pistol toward the gang.

Clye nodded, turned to face the crowd of shadowed outlaws. He holstered his pistol, but kept his hand on the grip. He cleared his throat.

"I've been an outlaw before. I understand your loyalty. Now Dayer promised that if I killed him you wouldn't kill me. Alright? Now if you stay in town I'll call the Law on you—"

"There is no Law," one of the outlaws piped up. "We killed every man with blue sewn onto his jacket."

Clye's stomach sank. "I see." He inhaled, tightened his grip around the handle of his pistol. "So what'll it be, boys? You leave me be and go on your way, or you satisfy your thirst for revenge and fight till the last man dies?"

The outlaw who had first spoken—a tall fellow in a bowler hat—pulled himself into the saddle of an imbval and glared out at Clye. "Proyton never dies. Tonight, we mourn our captain. Tomorrow, we burn this city to the ground." The man smiled. "And on and on, till the Law and Congress and skeletons in the mountains bow before Proyton Gang. We turn this world from law and poverty into freedom and prosperity. That is Proyton Gang, the everlasting."

He gave a shout—something guttural in a language Clye didn't recognize—and all the gang took it up. They charged past Clye, steering around him in two streams and merging together again. Clye stood still, his jaw set, flinching only twice as the steeds kicked up rocks and sand as they passed.

When the dust cleared, Clye turned to Kobe. "We gotta find some messengers—mailmen would do. Bring in some law-men from the other towns—maybe Congress." Clye put his hand to his face, winced when bloody bits of sand fell out of his wound. "Sandwalker help us."

## SIXTEEN
# HONOR BACK TO JUTE

IT TOOK SOME CONVINCING, but the messengers had gone out to Valkar and Capital Young with urgent pleas to the lawmen there.

This morning, they had arrived—ten lawmen, all rough-haired, well-spoken men from Valkar. Congress had been silent.

Clye stood in the town square, his back to the gallows, flanked on either side by the lawmen. Esta was there as well—she'd made Kobe stay behind and watch over Jerimiah.

They'd made all the preparations—ripped the market apart for the canvas, rounded up a few citizens to dip the cloth in water and cover what buildings they could. They hadn't convinced any of the citizens to fight—they all remained huddled in the inn and saloon, drinking the late Hollin Wesner's liquor. The cooks hadn't stuck around to defend it—they hung up their aprons and left town like angoraeths abandoning their eggs.

Clye wondered why none of them fought for their town. Was Jute such a dump that they didn't care to defend it? And yet they stayed, most of them. Huddled, drinking—waiting.

Something bound them to Jute, but it was not so strong that they would risk a life for it.

Clye scratched the stubble on his chin, glanced at the lawmen around him. Funny outlaw and lawmen should work together. But now it was just a matter of waiting—waiting for Proyton to strike a blow for their master and tear this poor town apart again. They didn't stand much of a chance, but if they survived, they would arrest the outlaws and pass judgment on them. Clye's throat constricted. *Have mercy*—he'd tell the lawmen that, when they took the outlaws in.

Esta stepped up beside Clye, her eyes fixed on the far end of the street that acted as channel between the square and the desert to the north. "What you thinkin'?"

Clye wrinkled his nose, watching a tumbleweed smack against the side of a building at the far end of the street. It bounced back, but the wind blew it once again to bounce against the wooden siding. Carried, struck, carried again. Clye exhaled. "I think I'm ready to go back."

"Back where?"

"Ranching," Clye breathed, tapping the lasso looped to his belt. "The Sandwalker freed me from the livin' hona of outlaw life—I'm ready to slow down, start my new life."

Esta pursed her lips. "We'll see, Mr. Galler."

"What's that?" one of the lawmen spoke up.

Clye squinted out at the desert. *Kein.* A massive dust cloud raced toward the town, surging and roiling like a mythical sea full of cackling dragons.

Clye clenched his jaw, winced a little when the scab split. He turned to the lawmen. "Alright, men," he said, "Let's fan out. Stay in the shelter of buildings with a bucket handy. Stick to the square like we'd planned—no sense in 'em pickin' us off by ones or twos. Sandwalker guard our lives."

"Valuk-va!" shouted the Valkar lawmen. Clye had no clue what it meant, but it sounded good.

Esta put a hand on Clye's shoulder, looked deep into his eyes with hers that were dark as the deep seas of myths. "Dead or alive," she said, "He'll be with you."

Clye's chest tightened. He nodded. "Dead or alive."

"Sandwalker guard your name," she let go of his shoulder and strode to the edge of the square, crouching down beside the well.

Clye inhaled. *Sandwalker guard my name...* The Sandwalker had redeemed it. He had saved this outlaw kive and turned him loose to protect this crooked town of Jute.

Clye glanced at the gathering dust cloud. It picked up speed as it neared the town, and spearheads poked from the top of the swirling sands. Clye strode over to the shadow of the blacksmith's shop at the west end of the square and crouched behind a pile of iron pots and wooden barrels.

The heaving mass of dust entered the mouth of the street, shaking the ground, hurling sand into the striped shops and stalls of the Jute market. Clye could see the hooves and heads of steeds as the storm began to slow, the outlaws atop them gripping spears and rifles, waving banners. The banners were of dusty-colored canvas, emblazoned with a dripping red curse. Most of the outlaws also carried burning torches.

Clye drew his revolver, aimed it at the approaching outlaws. There were thirty, at least—it was hard to count with all the dust. A tall outlaw in a bowler hat charged forward into the square on an imbval. Sand poured from the folds of his shirt and jacket. In his hand he gripped a polearm bearing one of those horrible banners.

"Proyton the everlasting!" he shouted, sweeping his gaze across the square.

A lawman crouching behind the gallows rose and fired without a word.

The tall outlaw toppled backward off his imbval with a hole in his head. The sand turned red with outlaw blood as his twisted corpse went still.

Clye clenched his jaw, resisted the urge to shoot the lawman. This was not the plan, shooting outlaws without warning.

The rest of the outlaws stopped on their steeds at the edge of the square, looking down at the body. The imbval whinnied and trotted back to the gang. The crowd of outlaws murmured together a moment under the wave of their torches.

Clye glanced over at Esta squatting beside the well. She nodded, fixed him with a gaze that said "Put a stop to this."

Clye inhaled. He stood up behind the stack of barrels, gripped his pistol tighter. "Proyton Gang!" he shouted, "We ain't here to kill you! If you throw down your arms we'll treat you with justice and civility. We ain't here to kill you."

But the outlaws didn't turn. They had finished their meeting, and began to pound their chests and fire a few rounds in the air, shouting ancient, guttural battle cries. With another whoop the whole pack of outlaws charged into the town square, fanning out, weapons brandished, beasts beneath them pounding the sand with their hooves.

They swarmed the gallows and Clye heard the moist cry of the lawman as they shot and stabbed him. A silent death repaid with a noisy one. Gunshots and cries rang out as the outlaws fanned out through the square. Two outlaws on wen-kiids charged toward Clye, their rifles lowered.

Clye gripped the sides of one of the big iron cauldrons and hauled it to the ground. Pistol in hand, he squatted down behind it, the tip of his hat peeking above the rim. Both outlaws fired. Clye bit his lip as one shot pinged off the cauldron and the other grazed the brim of his hat.

Clye raised his pistol as the outlaws reined in their beasts—just short of the shop's awning. He wanted to be out in the fight—out there to keep more of his friends from dying. If he could wrangle one of those wenkiids, he might have a chance out there.

One of the outlaws dismounted. The other remained mounted, just outside the shop. Beyond him in the square, gunshots exploded and the air was filled with the acid reek of imbval blood.

The outlaw who had dismounted swiveled his rifle toward Clye. Clye shot the man in the leg before he could make a move. The outlaw screamed, dropping to the ground and hugging his knee to his chest.

"Shoot the kive!" he cried to his fellow outlaw. The sounds of chaos in the town square were growing louder.

Without a word, the mounted outlaw slid off his wenkiid, cocking his rifle the moment he hit the ground. He fired at the cauldron. Clye held his hat, biting his lip against the ear-splitting sound of bullet on metal.

Clye could hear the injured outlaw shuffling where he lay on the ground, scrabbling in the sand for his rifle. Clye's heartbeat quickened. *Now or never.*

He exhaled, gripped his pistol, and leaped out from behind the iron pot. A gunshot went off, splintering into the closed door of the blacksmith's shop. Clye crossed the distance between him and the uninjured outlaw, the wenkiids clucking madly as he did.

The outlaw cocked his rifle, and Clye dove for his feet. He slammed into the man's legs, toppling him over as the gun went off. Clye scrambled atop the outlaw, shoving the rifle aside and slamming the hilt of his pistol against the man's head. The outlaw shuddered and went limp.

Clye holstered his pistol, glanced around the square. Outlaws and lawmen shot at each other from behind barrels, porches, and the stone gallows, several bodies of men and beasts staining the ground with their blood. The smell of gunpowder in the air was suffocating.

Clye heard the click of a rifle being cocked. He spun around. The injured outlaw lay on the ground, rifle raised awkwardly at Clye.

"Kein!" Clye dove under the shadow of the wenkiid as the gun went off. The beast clucked above him—Clye could feel its uneasiness. It was time for his final move.

Clye crawled out from under the wenkiid, jumped up and caught a stirrup. The creature hissed, spinning round, its neck craning to snap Clye in its beaked jaws. Clye grit his teeth, held on with all he had. Dust swirled as gunshots split the air. Clye hauled himself into the saddle, out of reach of the creature's lithe neck.

"Shh, shh..." Clye soothed, rubbing the soft part of the wenkiid's neck as it thrashed. The beast's movements slowed, and it calmed. Clye smiled. He looked out on the square. Some of the outlaws' torches had been cast, and the Law House was in flames. Clye swallowed and pulled out his revolver. *Time to get to work.*

Esta caught his eye as she ran for cover in the east end of the square. "Nice steed, cowboy!" she said.

Clye smiled. *Cowboy.*


THE SMOKE BILLOWED UP SOFTLY from the blackened roof of the Law House. The steps to the door had been ripped apart, partly black with soot and partly red with the day-old blood of Jute's lawmen. *They say a lawman's blood is worth a pint of gold.* Clye wondered why it was only theirs that was worth so much.

Sand was piled in banks against buildings and clogging the side-streets that led off from the square. The stone gallows were all that remained untouched, crimson rope still swinging, mocking the death around it when death was all it lived for.

"Terrible, ain't it." The Valkar lawman shook his head from side to side, gaze seeming to pause over every broken stone and burnt timber.

Clye nodded, arms crossed, his face shaded by his blood-red cowboy hat. He sighed. "We did what we could."

They had only lost three men—the rest were bunking at the K'maek Hotel without charge. Esta had gone home.

The lawman twirled his black mustache, turned to face Clye. His brown eyes looked sad in the shade of his broad-brimmed hat. "I'm sorry we couldn't have spared more men. If we had—"

"Proyton ain't that easy," Clye shook his head. He tried to keep his eyes from the burnt bodies that littered the ruins of Jute. "We have to build up a defense against 'em—keep the towns safe. Maybe they've left Jute for good, but Crayridge, Valkar, Capital Young—they're next."

The lawman snorted. "We killed half of them. The rest fled south like frightened snakes."

"They'll be back, bet your hat on it."

"Regardless." The lawman put a weathered hand on Clye's shoulder and smiled. "You've helped save Jute today. You should go home and rest—my fellow lawmen will sort things out here in town." He chewed on his lip, then, "You know what made Proyton strike a second time?"

"I killed their leader."

The lawman frowned. "What possessed you to do that?"

Clye paused. "He challenged me to a duel."

"*Proyton?*" The lawmen's eyes widened, then narrowed. "What's your name, son?"

"Clye Galler."

The lawmen stroked his mustache with his free hand. The hand on Clye's shoulder gripped tighter. "I feel like I recognize your face."

Clye pulled his shoulder away. "Many think all sons of Bu'rone look alike."

The lawman nodded. "Well, you take a rest for a while. We'll start a council to rebuild this town—bring peace and justice. Honor back to Jute." He clenched his fist.

Clye thought it strange he was so passionate since he'd only been in Jute a few hours.

The lawman spoke. "We might ask you to help us with that when you're back in town. That sound fine?"

"I'll think about it," Clye said, backing up, bowing, and turning to leave the square. He hoped he never would be back in town. Not while this lawman was in charge. Something about his eyes.

A WEEK WENT BY. Clye stayed at Esta's ranch, recovering from his wounds and caring for her beasts. They talked little of the battle—only answering Jerimiah's questions.

The evening was quiet, the wind softly hissing over the desert sands. Clye leaned against the railing of the porch, his stomach full of a good supper.

The door creaked open. Clye turned to see it was Esta, her cowboy hat sweeping around her gray brow like a crown.

She stopped, looked at him, hands on her hips. "Mr. Galler."

Clye raised an eyebrow.

"I saw that wenkiid you wrangled last week." A smile split her wrinkled face. "Outlaw wenkiid. Fast. On grains."

Clye shrugged. "It was calm enough."

"It's been nice havin' you around," Esta looked down at her tall boots, "but I cain't keep you around any longer. Wouldn't be fair."

"I can work harder for you," Clye said, "Jerimiah's cooking is more payment than I deserve. I can—"

"Mr. Galler." Esta furrowed her brow, extending her hand. "You're a cowboy."

Clye's breath caught in his chest. He quickly shook her hand. "I'm a cowboy?"

Esta nodded. "You've earned it. Wrangling an outlaw wenkiid in the heat of battle—that's something only a cowboy can do. Now run off. You pick out a steed, you head to the Law House and get a ranching license. Tell them Esta Galthor advocates for you."

Clye's heartbeat quickened. A cowboy. The job of his dreams. His pa would be proud. Clye tipped his hat. "Thank you, ma'am."

## SEVENTEEN
# THE COWBOY

THE COWBOY STRODE into the town square, his blood-red hat pulled down over his eyes, a revolver fitted into the holster on his hip, and a lasso looped around his belt.

The wind hissed over the sand, blowing drifts into the broken and burnt houses that lined the narrow street.

The cowboy crossed the square, but paused as he came to the stone gallows standing like an altar to Death in the afternoon sun. The heavy crimson rope creaked eerily.

On the far end of the square, the crooked Law House rose, half-burnt, with windows missing like the broken teeth of a skull.

The cowboy strode up to the door, noted that a rock had been placed beneath it where the old wooden steps had been. He could hear voices coming from between the cracked slats of the building. He didn't listen close, but the word "justice" was repeated several times.

The cowboy planted his leather boot embossed with the snake motif on the rock. He pulled up the other, and opened the door.

Inside, a round table sat in the center of the room with four or five lawmen seated around it. They had probably hauled the table in from the saloon, but the cowboy couldn't imagine how they got it in through the narrow door without snapping the legs off. The other lawmen must have been out on patrol.

The cowboy stood in the doorway a moment, then tapped his foot on the stone floor, cleared his throat.

A lawmen with a black mustache—the one who had talked to the cowboy a week ago—rose in his seat.

He wore no smile today. "Howdy," he said, teeth gritted, "Howdy, Mr. Yeller."

Clye inhaled, straightened, then let the breath out. *It's all right*, he told himself. "I'm sorry, sir, that's not my name. I'm *Galler*, not Yeller. I'm—"

"You *were* Yeller," the lawman hissed.

Clye knit his eyebrows together. "But now I'm not. Sheriff Quave cleared my name a couple weeks ago." He pulled the record paper out of his pocket.

The lawman sniffed at it. "Sheriff Quave is dead."

"The Law ain't."

The lawman smirked. "No indeed. The Law is up and alive and thirsting for justice—true justice, Yeller. The justice where men die for their deeds and outlaws don't go free." He had risen from his chair. "The justice where the blame always falls, and honor always wins. Mr. Yeller, why did you kill Dayer Proyton? Why did you anger the gang so that they demolished this already withering town?"

Clye put his hand to his hip. "I'm a cowboy, sir, not an outlaw. I came here to get my ranching license. Esta Galthor advocates for me."

The lawman stopped. He had circled the table, now stood only a yard or so from the cowboy. He crossed his arms. "Get that outlaw."

Instantly, all five lawmen leaped up, pistols brandished. Before the cowboy could turn around to flee, they were on him. A bullet through the knee, a scream, then ropes around wrists and a drop of blood on the floor.

Then the lawman's voice, droning, "Lyle Yeller, outlaw, for murder, for lying, for the destruction of Jute, I sentence you to hang upon the morrow in the town square…"

A fist in the face. All went black.


CLYE FOUND HIMSELF lying on the floor of the prison cell, face pressed to the warm stone. His knee throbbed with pain. He could feel ropes wrapped around his now bare feet. Grains coated his face, stuck to his eyelashes. Sunlight filtered in through every slat in the wall and empty window, searching for something to pry at, to stab, to expose. Clye looked along the floor, through the iron bars untouched by Proyton's destruction. Across the stone floor, past Sheriff Quave's old desk, in the dusty corner beside the door, an envelope sat, light glancing off the wax seal—as red as blood from a hanged outlaw's mouth.

Clye sighed. His wonderful pa, his difficult ma—both gone. There was no more love or pain that they could give him. Death hurt, whether it was pain or love that it was cutting short. Clye would never get to read their letter—hear their words once more before he met his own end.

A lawman shifted in his seat at the table. They had only left one guard to watch Clye until the hanging—the ropes around his wrists and feet and the bullet in his knee were guards enough.

Clye closed his eyes. His parents hadn't saved him. His cleared name hadn't saved him. Only the Sandwalker had saved him.

The days since the Sands had not been without pain—or failure. Clye's chest tightened as his memory flitted back to the dark afternoon in the bottom of the mine—so much death. The duel with Dayer—more death.

And now he would face his own death.

No one would save him—Esta had released him of his duty, and would not expect to see him for some time. Hollin, Ma, Pa, Jen, Quave—all dead. There was no stopping his hanging this time.

Hanging is for the guilty. Clye had been guilty, plenty. But he had been cleared—legally, and in his heart. Why now? Why was he being hanged when he had been cleared?

The door creaked open. Clye opened his eyes. He saw the Valkar lawman crossing the room, stopping beside the table.

"Lyle Yeller," he said, "get ready for Hona."

Clye bit his lip, shut his eyes. He felt the tremor of the cell door unlocking, heard the deathly scrape of it opening. He felt the arms hauling him to his feet.

"Sandwalker," he said, "thank you for keeping the blood within my body, the heart within my chest, the dreams within my eyelids, and guarding my name with your whirlwinds."

A tear fell from his eye.

THEY DRAGGED THE COWBOY out into the afternoon sun. A small crowd had gathered, arms crossed, faces expressionless. There was no bloodlust here—no cheering crowd waiting to be entertained. These were people crushed, broken, with naught but the Law to lean on.

The lawmen cut the ropes binding the cowboy's feet, propped him up on the hot stone around the gallows' base while they declared his sentence.

The Minister was there in the crowd. The lawmen offered to let him lead the hat-burning ceremony. He refused.

The Valkar lawman took the cowboy's blood-red hat, and pulled a torch that was already burning around the gallows' stone base. The hat ignited, turning to smoke and ashes like the broken town the lawman was now leading.

They set the cowboy upon the stone pillar rising beneath the swinging red rope. Was this justice? To kill a man forgiven twice over? They set the noose around the cowboy's neck. His crimes had been egregious. Steed-theft, murder, and provoking the most dangerous gang in Drode. His past was blacker than the stone his bare feet were gripping.

They put no bag over his head, no cloth in his mouth to stop the blood. When they pulled the lever and the stone pillar fell away, one of the bystanders whispered to another, "They say the life of an outlaw ain't worth a pint of milk, but who says? Who decides?"

"I don't know, hona." The other dabbed his eye with a kerchief. "What if we all died for our sins?"

The first bystander shook his head. "Don't think our blood is worth that much."

They let the cowboy's body roast to bones on the hot sands of the desert. Clye Galler was a fiend, most said. Others said he was a man of honor—broken, forgiven. Who can say which were right? Ghosts would know, but the myths say they lie.

Help other readers find great literature.

Will you take one minute right now and leave an honest, one-sentence review of *Outlaw Blood* on Amazon or Goodreads?

———————

# AUTHOR'S
# NOTE

WHEN I WAS ten years old I decided to become a writer.

My plan was simple—write a book and toddle up to the front desk at Zondervan and get a meeting with their "making books person." I'd read the book out loud to them, they'd print thousands of copies, and I'd parade the streets in sunglasses drinking fame like booze.

Turns out that's not how publishing works.

Turns out it looks more like showing up every day to write words, revise words, post words on social media, and show those words to the right people who can help you make those words better and maybe (maybe) publish those words.

I'm one of the lucky ones.

I know my publisher personally. He's my mentor.

You could say that this whole thing is just an elaborate school assignment.

Which is true.

But also, it's more than that.

This is a foray into the depths of publishing. This is a desperate attempt to throw my first batch of chum at the water and see if the sharks come up (that's you—the awesome reader—by the way).

And even more than all that, this is me making up words with Jesus to see if some of them—maybe—hit a desperate heart out there.

To see if some of them—perhaps—raise an eyebrow, turn a head.

To see if some of them—maybe—hit something deep and mean something to someone out there.

Will they?

I don't pretend to know.

That's not my job.

My job is to show up and bleed in front of the computer every day to bless the world with entertainment that means something.

My job is to call people to pursue the best that God has for them.

The life of an outlaw may only be worth a pint of milk, but your life? God thought that was worth dying for.

Your life is worth God's blood.

Chew on that.

Now let a little of that blood—that life—into the world. You have a dream, and when you grab it with both hands and let it take you where God wants, it'll make the world better.

The world needs to see your dream.

Open your veins, and bleed some life into this world.

I hope that's what I've done here.

# ACKNOWLEDGMENTS

IN SOME ABSTRACT WAYS this book has been ten years in the making. In other more concrete ways it's only been one year in the making.

Whichever it is, there's been a massive number of people who've made this possible.

First off I want to thank my mentor, Brad Pauquette. You're the one who reached out to me two years ago with the million-dollar question: "Why don't you apply for the apprenticeship this year?"

Scared the heck out of me; in more ways than one, I suppose.

I've never grown as much as I have under you at The Company—I can't even begin to express my gratitude. If they measured impact in inches, you've ringed the world of Drode thrice over. God bless you and your amazing family.

I also want to thank my family—Mom, Dad, Levi, Judah, Abigail, Josephine, Sam, Ezra, and Ruby—you guys have been the best. So fun. So supportive. So patient.

Mom, you're an amazing homeschool teacher. The way you taught us to learn and pursue our dreams is what's made all this possible.

Dad, you've been so wise and I'm so glad you sat me down at the Grayling restaurant and encouraged me to say yes to God's calling.

Levi, be happy with your cover.

And if I wrote a personal message to all of you we'd have another book on our hands so I'll save the poor readers the hassle and summarize—you are my favorite-est, wonderful-est siblings. You're all so funny and I'm so glad to be your big brother. Say hi to Bob Quantum for me.

I also want to thank everyone at Wally's Pizza and Subs—I can pay rent because of you.

Huge thanks to the whole production crew who brought this book to life—Vella Karman, R.J. Catlin, Brad Pauquette (again), Levi Matthews, and Thirzah. This book would be a disaster without you guys.

Shoutout to the other students at The Company—Rebekah, Alli, Vella, Lucy—you guys have been so encouraging through my journey. The number of times you all have fed me, encouraged me, and let me cry at your house is probably limitless at this point. I'm so thankful to you all. You've been such real friends.

And before this list becomes miles long, I'd like to thank my BFF Sam Van Slyke. Make your movies, bro—I'll catch up when the writing thing takes off.

And finally, I want to thank Jesus.

For all the crap I've done to You, You still love me. I want to be more like You.

# ABOUT
# THE AUTHOR

NOAH J. MATTHEWS is an author and aspiring filmmaker from the backwoods of Northern Michigan.

Currently based in Ohio, he's lucky he's not a Michigan fan. Otherwise, you might see his head on a pike somewhere by the side of an Appalachian highway.

Noah is a Star Wars nerd, recovering C. S. Lewis addict, and hopeless lover of Jesus.

Noah's calling is to entertain and challenge people with artful media, while at the same time inspiring them to pursue the dreams God has placed on their lives.

You can find him at his website NoahJMatthews.com, where he regularly blogs about how to get serious about your calling and bring your dreams into reality.

# Don't stop now.
## There's more like *Outlaw Blood*.

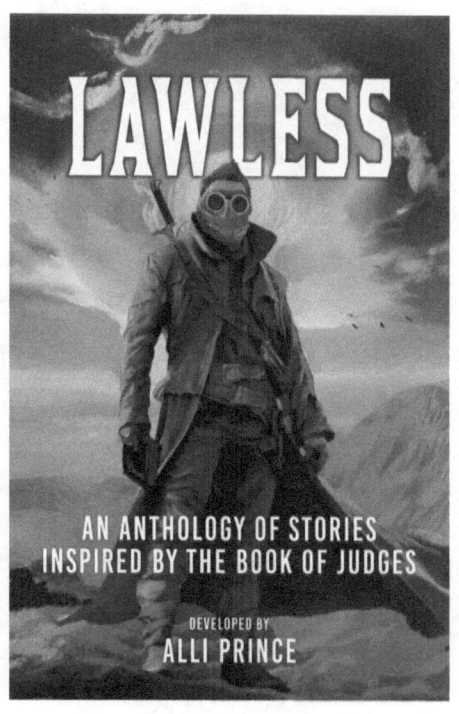

Enjoy the work of Alli Prince and Brad Pauquette, with twelve other authors, in this gritty, imaginative, western sci-fi anthology based on the biblical book of Judges.

Available wherever great books are sold!
**LawlessBook.com**

Scan for Amazon

# Ready to write like Noah?

Noah J. Matthews is a second-year apprentice at The Company. If you're ready to kick your writing into gear and make cool stuff, check it out at:

**Writers.Company**

---

## Better than "Christian" literature.
### More great stories are just around the corner.

New short stories, essays, and poetry published weekly. Read and subscribe today at

**PearlMag.co**